*Lord, please. I kno
lives or dies, but p
Please.*

Jake rushed across the room and stood over her. She blinked a few times and seemed almost lucid.

"Who are you?" she asked, her voice sounding thick and heavy. Then her eyes widened. "Kelly!"

"She's fine and right here." Jake held the baby up for Rachael to see.

"Thank You, sweet Jesus," Rachael whispered, her words slurred. "You were looking out for us."

Her lips tipped in a sweet smile, and Jake's heart leaped. Despite the medics standing by, he couldn't seem to pull his gaze from hers.

"We should get her and the baby transported," the medic said, ruining the moment.

"We're going with you." Jake reluctantly pulled away and settled Kelly in her carrier, then glanced back at Rachael. He wasn't sure if Kelly or Rachael looked more vulnerable.

Didn't matter, now did it?

He wasn't going to let anything bad happen to either of them. He'd make sure they were both protected until he was certain that neither of them remained in danger.

Susan Sleeman is a bestselling author of inspirational and clean-read romantic suspense books and mysteries. She received an RT Reviewers' Choice Best Book Award for *Thread of Suspicion*. *No Way Out* and *The Christmas Witness* were finalists for the Daphne du Maurier Award for Excellence. She's had the pleasure of living in nine states and currently lives in Oregon. To learn more about Susan, visit her website at susansleeman.com.

Books by Susan Sleeman

Love Inspired Suspense

First Responders

Silent Night Standoff
Explosive Alliance
High-Caliber Holiday
Emergency Response
Silent Sabotage
Christmas Conspiracy

The Justice Agency

Double Exposure
Dead Wrong
No Way Out
Thread of Suspicion
Dark Tide

High-Stakes Inheritance
Behind the Badge
The Christmas Witness
Holiday Defenders
"Special Ops Christmas"

Visit the Author Profile page at Harlequin.com.

CHRISTMAS CONSPIRACY

SUSAN SLEEMAN

HARLEQUIN® LOVE INSPIRED® SUSPENSE

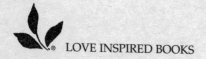 LOVE INSPIRED BOOKS

Recycling programs for this product may not exist in your area.

ISBN-13: 978-0-373-44784-8

Christmas Conspiracy

www.Harlequin.com

Printed in U.S.A.

Therefore do not worry about tomorrow, for tomorrow will worry about itself. Each day has enough trouble of its own.
—Matthew 6:34

For the beautiful daughter I lost in miscarriage.
I know heaven smiled the day you arrived.

ONE

Hot, ugly eyes stared at Rachael from black circles in the gunman's mask. If he planned to kill her, he needed to do it quickly or she would fight him to the last breath. She'd rather die than see him hurt a child under her care.

She straightened her shoulders and checked on Kelly, asleep in her crib at Rachael's child development center. Oblivious to the threat, the precious three-month-old pushed her fist under her chin, and soft breaths pursed her lips. She was helpless and depended on Rachael for protection.

The gunman took another step.

Rachael backed up and draped all five feet five inches of her body across the front of Kelly's crib. "You'll have to go through me to get to her. I might be small, but I'll put up a fight."

"Don't be a fool." He jerked his gun toward the wall with brightly painted cubbies holding the belongings of the six infants cared for in this room. "Step away from the baby. I don't want to hurt you, but I will if I have to."

Rachael didn't comply, but memorized his voice—the inflection, the slight rasp. If he got away and left her alive, she could help identify him. But first, she needed to make sure she and Kelly lived.

Rachael tightened her hands on the crib rail, connecting with the solid maple and holding on for dear life. "I'm not moving."

His eyes narrowed. "Then we do this the hard way."

"Or you could not do this at all," she suggested, but he ignored her and took long steps across the room.

Dressed in black, he stood six feet tall and had an athletic build. He wore latex gloves and brandished the gun like he'd held one before. He stepped off and she waited, her eyes fixed on his weapon, expecting it to discharge.

Step by step, he moved across the brightly colored area rug with teddy bears and bunnies that she'd chosen when she'd opened the center three years ago. Never in her wildest dreams had she expected a masked man, intent on kidnapping a precious little baby, would cross this rug.

"Please, don't do this," Rachael begged.

He ignored her and kept coming, crossing the room. *Thump. Thump. Thump.* His hiking boots pounded on the gleaming linoleum, the gun still outstretched in his hands.

Her confidence wavered, and her palms grew moist, the solid rail becoming slick under her hands. Panic stole her breath, and she fought to draw in another one.

Stay calm. Kelly needs you.

The gunman slowed, then stopped in front of her and fixed those burning eyes on hers while pressing the barrel of his gun to her forehead. "Are you ready to cooperate now?"

Fear coursed through her chest, and her hands trembled, but she held her position. Another child's life wouldn't end on her watch. The guilt of losing another innocent baby would tear her apart.

She gave a small shake of her head, feeling the gun barrel cold against her skin.

"Fine." He clamped his free hand on her forearm and spun her swiftly, then snaked his arm around her chest, pinning her arms at her sides and clutching her tight against his body.

The gun no longer at her head, Rachael arched her back and bucked.

His arm held like a vise, tightening, crushing down and bruising her flesh.

She cried out in pain and instantly hated that she'd let him know he'd hurt her.

"You wanted it this way." He laid his gun on the mattress near Kelly's sleeper-covered feet before using that hand to dig through his jacket pocket.

The sight of his gun lying so close to Kelly hit Rachael like a physical punch to her gut.

How had this happened? No—how had she let this happen?

As the center's owner and director, she held the responsibility for Kelly while her mother, Pam, worked. Rachael had wanted to help Pam out today when she'd had to go to work early or risk losing her job, so Rachael had taken Kelly before the center opened. She'd thought it would be fine, but then the first teacher of the day got a flat tire, leaving Rachael alone. And now she'd failed Pam. Failed Kelly.

Rachael had to find a way to save the sweet baby.

But what could she do? She'd already tried everything she could think of. This man wanted Kelly, and he didn't care what he had to do to get her.

Lord, please. Stop this now, she prayed. *Don't let him take Kelly.*

She waited for a bit of calm, maybe peace, but none came. Nothing odd about that. She hadn't felt true peace since she'd lost her husband and unborn child four years ago. Tears rolled down her cheeks and dropped to the crib, landing on the pastel teddy bears covering the mattress.

Kelly shifted, drawing her pudgy little legs up tighter under her body.

"I'm so sorry, Kelly," Rachael whispered.

Her captor tightened his grip while continuing to fumble around behind her. She slowly leaned toward the crib and slid her fingers closer to the gun. Inch by inch she moved. Closer. Closer.

Almost there.

He jerked his hand free of his pocket and karate chopped her forearm. "Don't even think about it."

"Please don't take Kelly," Rachael begged as a raw ache radiated up her arm.

He ignored her again, shifted to the side, and a sharp pain pierced her arm.

What? He'd injected her with something.

"Don't worry." His minty fresh breath crept through her hair as he clamped his arms tighter around her. "When you wake up, I'll be long gone. Of course, so will Kelly. Have a nice nap now."

No! She had to get free.

She roared like a fierce mother bear with a threatened cub and put all of her strength into one last attempt. But his arms felt like bands of steel, and she couldn't break free.

"Shh," he said. "Just give it a few minutes and you won't care anymore. The drug is a powerful anesthetic. Takes away all your worries and fears before you sleep. Peaceful, sweet sleep."

Time seemed to stand still, but Rachael didn't. She fought hard until the drug he'd put into her body sent waves of relaxation through her muscles.

She whimpered. "Please, I'll do anything. Give you money. Anything. Don't take Kelly."

"Don't fight the drug," he said. "You'll soon be asleep, and all of this will be over."

Her body grew heavy, and it took effort just to keep her head up. He backed away from the crib. Her body flopped like a rag doll as he lowered her to the floor and rolled her onto her back. She had one last chance, one more to save Kelly.

Rachael dug deep, beyond the waves of comfort that were flowing through her body, and shot her arm up to jerk off his mask.

His mouth dropped open as he gaped at her in horror. He cursed, but she ignored his words and memorized every pore on his face. A wide jaw. Whiskered chin. Jet-black hair to go with his cold gray eyes. High cheekbones. A mole near his left ear. She'd never seen him before, but she'd be able to describe him to the police.

"I've seen you now," she said, her words slurring. "You won't get away with this."

Her arm fell to the floor, and she dropped his mask.

Her mind clouded, and her strength receded. He retrieved his mask and put it back on, then continued to glare at her. Her eyes blinked closed. She forced them open. Dizziness swept in like a tidal wave. Her muscles liquefied. She felt as if her body floated toward the ceiling.

"I have no choice now," he finally growled out. "I'll have to kill you."

Kill me? Okay. That was fine. Everything was fine. The peace she'd sought a moment ago descended in an ocean of joy.

Yes, this was better. Nothing was wrong. Nothing mattered.

Her head fell to the side. Her gaze caught on Kelly's crib. Precious three-month-old Kelly. Asleep. Like the heaviness pulling Rachael down.

Kelly.

Rachael's thoughts drifted.

Wasn't there a reason she should be concerned about the baby?

Four years of denied sleep beckoned. Her eyelids drooped.

She lay on the floor. Blinking. Floating. Trying to remember what was happening.

As if he had all the time in the world, he sauntered toward her, his boots thumping on the floor.

Rachael tried to lift her hand. So heavy. She willed her eyes to remain open to see what he might be planning, but her eyelids closed like the lid on a casket, and soon, she knew nothing at all.

"It's looking like the kidnapper's really going to kill her." Jake Marsh, commander of the First Response Squad, stared at the live video feed of director Rachael Long and the gunman in the Columbia Child Development Center.

Jake and two members of the FRS had been on their way to a tactical training session in their command truck when dispatch rerouted them to the center. Thankfully, many child care centers streamed live video so parents at work could see their children. As soon as the call came in, his team had easily accessed the feed, and they now watched the action from their command truck.

The kidnapper slipped the baby's arms into a snow-suit then strapped her into the infant seat. Taking great care with the baby, he struggled with the straps. Jake had no children, but he knew it almost took a college degree these days to figure out how to properly use a car seat, buying the team time to intercept him.

"The director got a good look at his face before he put the mask back on, so there's no way he's going to let her live," Jake said. "Too bad the camera angles aren't giving us a look at his face, but I guess it doesn't matter right now. We just need to get in there quickly."

"If whatever he injected her with hasn't already killed her." Team sniper Brady Owens looked up from behind the video console, an ominous look on his face.

"We don't have any time to lose," Cash Dixon, their bomb expert, said.

Jake nodded. "We'll proceed as if this is a hostage rescue. Cash, you remain here and monitor communications. Brady, let's move!"

Jake charged out the door, wishing negotiators Skyler Hunter and Archer Reed were with them. As squad leader, Jake had needed to act as negotiator only twice in the six years he'd directed the team.

Well, today will be your third, and a baby's and woman's lives depend on you. No pressure.

He stifled his concerns and took a good look around. Not even 7:00 a.m., the sun hadn't yet climbed into the sky. Warm light spilled from the center's windows, sparkling off the recent snowfall, but Jake's attention went to an empty patrol car sitting in the lot.

Brady stepped up behind him. "What's a patrol car doing here?"

"My question exactly," Jake replied.

"Likely some hotshot who ignored directives to stand down."

Brady sucked in a breath. "The guy's gonna get himself or the woman killed."

"Just picked up the deputy on video," Cash said over

Jake's earpiece. "He's in the hallway outside the baby room."

"Then negotiations are off the table, and we're going in strong." Jake mentally called up the center's blueprint he'd viewed in the truck.

A main hall ran down the middle of the building. Doors for classrooms and a kitchen faced that hall. Each room had at least one exit leading to playgrounds behind the tall fence. The baby room was the second room on the south side of the building, with two exterior doors.

Jake shifted his steel-plated tactical vest. "Cash, keep us updated on any movements."

"Roger that," Cash said.

Jake started forward as sharp winds howled down the Columbia River, sending trees rustling. Directly ahead sat a fenced yard with two gates—and one of them stood open. Jake held up a hand and paused to check for any sign of danger.

Finding none, he peered at Brady. "I'll intercept the deputy in the hallway. You hold at the side entrance to the baby room."

"Affirmative," Brady replied before moving swiftly toward the open gate.

Jake approached the front door. A fragrant pine wreath with a red Christmas bow caught his attention for but a moment. He turned the doorknob. Entered. Paused again.

Darkness obscured the hallway, but light escaped from under the baby room door and through the window. The wayward deputy stood looking through the window, but he hadn't yet opened the door.

"Stand down," Jake announced loud enough for the deputy to hear but, he hoped, not loud enough for his voice to carry into the baby room.

The deputy spun, his weapon raised. He hadn't rotated fully when he fired.

Bam. Bam.

The bullets slammed into Jake's vest. The crushing force felt like a baseball bat to the chest, pushing him back and knocking him to the floor while stealing his breath. His first instinct had his hand going to the Velcro to rip off his vest, gain a breath and ease the pain, but the kidnapper would have heard the shots and could open the door and fire off a few rounds.

"Oh, man," the deputy cried out and ran to Jake. "Man, I didn't... I mean you're..."

"Shooter spooked by shots fired," Brady announced over the comms.

"Roger that," Jake managed to get out as he continued to fight for air. "Make entry now."

"Affirmative," Brady replied.

The deputy dropped down beside Jake. Jake glared at the guy and wanted to give him a piece of his mind, but he wouldn't waste any more time on the deputy. Not when Brady counted on Jake for backup.

He struggled to his feet, his anger barely in check. He should have been the one to breach the perimeter. He was in charge. He was the best trained. He should have taken the risk. Thanks to the yo-yo staring at him, Jake had lost all control of this op. Losing control meant people died.

Boom. Boom. Boom.

The shots sounded from a handgun inside the room. Brady carried a rifle, which meant the masked man had opened fire. Jake listened for Brady's return fire.

Nothing.

The kidnapper could have taken Brady out, or maybe Brady took cover and didn't have a shot. Either way, Jake had to get inside.

He eyed the deputy. "Go back to your car and don't leave it until you're told to do so. You got me?"

He nodded.

"Now!"

Jake waited for him to step off, then bolted for the door.

"Entering," Jake said into his mic as he jerked open the door to find Brady, rifle raised, his concentration on the sight as he marched toward the back door.

"Got in just in time to draw the kidnapper's fire," he called out. "His shots went wide. Missed the director. He fired on me and took off with the baby. I had to take cover. Couldn't get a clean shot without risking the baby's life."

Jake wished Brady could have taken the shot, but as an extremely capable deputy, if he said there hadn't been a clean shot, then no shot existed.

Jake glanced at the director. She lay on her back, but she stirred, and her eyes blinked open. Her gaze met Jake's for a moment before they closed again. He wanted to check on her, but the baby took priority right now.

At least he knew Brady had been wrong in the truck. They weren't too late, and Ms. Long was alive.

Now Jake needed to make sure she stayed that way.

TWO

Jake charged to the door, his chest aching like crazy, but with lives on the line, his pain didn't matter. Finding the baby was what mattered now. He moved forward, caution in his steps, and scanned the playground. Mulch crunched under his feet near the pint-size playground structure, and the gate ahead swung in the breeze.

He wanted to burst through the opening, but that would be foolhardy, so he paused and swept the area. A larger playground in the distance held a tall play structure with a thick layer of mulch in the fall zone. A six-foot fence surrounded the area and Brady, rifle slung over his shoulder, scaled the fence boards.

"Report," Jake said into his mic.

Brady didn't lose a beat at the command but hurled over the top. "Kidnapper went over the fence here. Couldn't take the baby."

Jake looked down and spotted the carrier sitting near the fence. The child squirmed and kicked her little feet. He let out a heavy sigh.

"Continue foot pursuit," Jake commanded. "I've got the baby."

He crossed the playground and directed his voice at his mic. "Cash, call in backup to track this guy, and get some uniforms on scene to set up a perimeter. We'll need a detective dispatched. Skyler has the best closure rate of county detectives, and I suspect she'll be assigned to the investigation, but give her a call so she has a heads-up and can ask to work the case."

"Roger that," Cash replied, and Jake knew he would immediately phone their teammate.

When not working as a negotiator on the FRS, Skyler served as a Special Investigations Unit detective, and since this case involved a young child, Jake wanted the best investigator on the job.

He crossed the yard and bent over to pick up the carrier. His chest screamed in agony. Of course. His adrenaline was subsiding, and the pain from the deputy's shots would grow by the minute.

The baby blinked her lashes at him, her eyes wide and interested when he'd expected tears. Some babies were good-natured, and nothing riled them. His little sister had been like that. All giggles and smiles, all the time. That could be true of this child.

Her smile widened into a toothless grin, and his pain receded. His team had done a good thing today. They'd successfully stopped the abduction of this little princess. That felt good. Real good.

She suddenly frowned and narrowed her tiny blue eyes, then screwed up her face like a wrinkled prune and started to whimper.

"Shh." He gently shook the carrier, mimicking motions he remembered from helping care for his brother and sister. "It's okay. You're safe, Kelly. At least that's what the director said your name was."

She didn't settle but wailed in earnest, flailing her arms and legs in her pink snowsuit. Jake stopped and stared at her for a long moment.

What in the world was he supposed to do with a crying baby?

He commanded an emergency response team, leading them into some of the most volatile and dangerous situations law enforcement deputies could encounter, but a baby, let alone one whose cry gave emergency sirens a run for their money, brought more fear to his heart than the toughest spots he'd been in.

He hadn't had any experience with babies since he'd lost both of his siblings when he was a mere kid himself, but he figured she wanted to be held. Or changed. Once they got inside, he'd hold her. But the other? No way. He wasn't about to attempt that.

To comfort her, he gently swung the carrier as he walked, each swing like a knife to his chest, but the motion served to slow the crying to a whimper. Inside, he found the director still unconscious on the floor. He hurried over to her, set down the carrier and knelt next to her. He released the carrier to lay two fingers on her wrist. Her pulse beat hard but her breathing seemed shallow.

"So, Rachael Long," he mumbled. "What did the guy inject you with?"

He wished Darcie Stevens, the team medic, had been with them. She possessed the training needed to enter a volatile situation and would already be tending to the director. Other medics didn't have such skills. They were required to wait until the suspect no longer posed a threat to their safety before treating Ms. Long.

Jake adjusted his mic. "Are there medics standing by, Cash?"

"Affirmative."

"Send them in as soon as you're sure it's safe." Jake rocked the carrier as he looked at Rachael.

The heater kicked in, sending a whiff of her sweet perfume wrapping around him and temporarily overpowering the antiseptic odor of bleach permeating the air. About five-five, she was small compared to his six-foot-two frame. She appeared fit, had curling, shoulder-length hair and freckles peppered high cheeks. She seemed sweet, almost innocent. Exactly what he'd expect of a child care director.

She wore a wedding ring, but preliminary information gathered as the team raced toward the scene told him she'd lost her husband in a car crash about four years ago, and she hadn't remarried.

Now she lay there. Near death? He wanted to do something to help.

He jumped to his feet and retrieved a few child-sized blankets from the cribs. He returned to cover her, then turned his attention to Kelly, whose cries had escalated. He ripped off his tactical gloves and took off his helmet, figuring it might be scaring her. Then he released her restraints and lifted her into his arms. The steel plates of his vest weren't likely comfortable, so he lowered her and held her slightly away from his body while he rocked back and forth.

"Shh," he whispered and listened to the chatter on his comms unit to keep updated on the chase.

The kidnapper had disappeared from Brady's view, so Cash had called in a search dog. Jake didn't get his hopes up, though. Since most properties were fenced in the city, and dogs often lost the scent at fence lines, odds were against them in locating the kidnapper.

Jake continued to listen while rocking the baby until she settled down and drifted to sleep. The front door opened, and the sound of gurney wheels finally echoed down the hallway.

Two men entered. The thin guy who stepped in first

wore a Santa hat. The other guy was bald and tough-looking, and Jake suspected he'd never worn a Santa hat in his life.

Jake stepped back to give them access to Rachael. "You up to speed on the incident?"

The guy with the hat knelt on the floor next to Rachael. "The woman was injected with something and is unconscious but breathing."

"Exactly," Jake replied.

"Dog has lost the scent," Brady said over Jake's earbuds, then reported his exact location.

"Widen the perimeter and stand ready," Jake replied. "We'll have to hope 911 receives a call reporting the kidnapper's movements."

And hope he doesn't harm anyone as he makes his escape.

"Roger that." Disappointment lingered in Brady's tone.

Suddenly weary beyond his thirty-five years, Jake ran a hand over tense muscles in his neck and watched the medics do their thing. Once they had an IV going, they loaded Rachael onto the gurney.

An overwhelming desire to protect her and Kelly from additional harm rose up and caught him off guard. He worked each callout with the thought that he would do everything he could so he didn't have to live with regret, but he'd never taken a personal interest in the people he rescued.

Until right now. But why?

Could have to do with losing his infant sister and six-year-old brother, he supposed. When he'd just turned thirteen, they, and his parents, perished in a bombing, leaving him with a soft spot in his heart for children in danger and the special people who cared for them. And a burning desire to see anyone who threatened them pay for their actions.

He glanced at Ms. Long on the gurney as the medics strapped her in, and her eyelids fluttered.

Lord, please. I know you decide who lives or dies, but please let this woman live. Please.

Jake crossed the room and stood over her. She blinked a few times and seemed almost lucid.

"Who are you?" she asked, her voice sounding thick and heavy. Then her eyes widened. "Kelly!"

"She's fine and right here." Jake held the baby up for Rachael to see.

"Thank you, sweet Jesus," Rachael whispered, her words slurred. "You were looking out for us."

Her lips tipped up in a sweet smile, and Jake's heart hesitated. Despite the medics standing by, he couldn't seem to pull his gaze from hers.

"We should get her and the baby transported," the medic said, ruining the moment.

"We're going with you." Jake reluctantly pulled away and settled Kelly in her carrier, then glanced back at Rachael. He wasn't sure if Kelly or Rachael looked more vulnerable.

Didn't matter, now, did it?

There was no way he'd let anything bad happen to either of them. He'd make sure they were both protected until he was certain that neither of them remained in danger.

Rachael saw the light flashing over her head before she opened her eyes. Bright fluorescent tubes wavered in and out of her view in squiggly lines. She concentrated harder and battled the residual fog from the drug.

She heard rushed, hurried voices in the distance.

Smelled the antiseptic of the hospital, reminding her she lay in a hard bed in the ER. She'd woken thirty minutes ago and talked to the doctor, but the drug's effects kept pulling her back under. She had to try harder to stay awake so she could talk to Pam and see Kelly.

She blinked hard and made an effort to clear her vision.

"She's awake," a deep male voice said from across the small room.

Did he mean her—and who *was* he, anyway?

She heard his footsteps as he came near, and she forced her head to turn toward the sound. The resulting wave of dizziness sent her stomach roiling. She blinked until she could focus on a large man wearing a black uniform now looking down on her.

"Ms. Long," he said softly, his face so familiar—but she was sure she didn't know him. "Can you hear me?"

"Yes," she replied.

"I'm Deputy Sergeant Jake Marsh. I was one of the deputies who found you unconscious in the baby room."

Ah, so that was who he was. She remembered him now. His kindness in the ambulance. Holding precious Kelly's carrier for the ride, safe and secure in his hands. He'd said a neighbor noticed the masked man enter the playground and called 911. He arrived to help and had chased off the kidnapper.

"Deputy," she said. "Yes. I remember you."

"Call me Jake."

"I'm Rachael."

"It's nice to see you're awake, Rachael." A dazzling smile broke across his face.

A little zip of awareness shot through her stomach, catching her off guard. She'd been only vaguely aware of him this far, as she hadn't been fully awake when he'd ridden along in the ambulance. Then after the medics rushed her into the ER, the staff forced him to wait outside her door, and she hadn't seen him since then.

He was a fine-looking man. Six foot two, maybe, muscled and brawny. Chocolate-brown eyes. Olive skin. Ebony hair. Yeah, he was a striking man, but why was she noticing? She'd been immune to men's charms after she married Eli. Especially immune after he died in the car accident that was all her fault, so where was the reaction to this guy coming from all of a sudden?

She was probably confusing this interest in him with gratitude for his rescue and protection. After all, he'd saved her life. Or maybe the drugs had caused her to let down her guard. Either way, she wouldn't waste time analyzing it when she doubted she'd ever see him again.

"Thank you for your help," she said.

He gave a clipped nod. "It was a team effort, and we were just doing our jobs."

His job. A dangerous and difficult job, she suspected. One she could never do, at least not if she hoped to sleep at night.

Scenes of the attempted kidnapping flooded her brain. Her fear. Her anger. Little Kelly, vulnerable. Everything came to her except details of the intruder's face. That she couldn't seem to call up from her memory. In the times she'd been awake, she'd tried to recall what he looked like, but only fuzzy images came to mind.

The doctor had told her that the police found an empty vial of ketamine on the floor at the center. Doctors and veterinarians used the drug for conscious sedation. He said as the drug left her system, she might remember the kidnapper in more detail, but the levels of drug in her blood meant she wouldn't likely recall much of anything after the ketamine had taken hold.

She might not remember the kidnapper's face, but she would never forget Kelly sleeping peacefully in her crib, danger lurking all around her.

"Is Kelly really okay?" She managed to get the words out through a mouth that felt like it was stuffed with cotton.

Jake smiled. "She's fine. She's with her mother."

A woman stepped around the deputy and displayed a wallet that held a shiny badge. "I'm Detective Skyler Hunter. I'll be handling this investigation, and if you're up to it, I have a few questions for you."

Rachael ran her gaze over the woman. She looked like she was an inch or so taller than Rachael, had red hair and wore khaki pants and a blue blazer. The lapel held a Christmas button that said Jesus Is the Reason for the Season.

Never having been questioned by the police, apprehension settled in Rachael's stomach, but the concern in the detective's expression seemed sincere and gave Rachael hope that the questioning wouldn't be too bad.

"You're the one who'll catch this terrible man, then?" Rachael asked.

"I'll do my very best, yes."

Rachael eased herself up on her pillows until she reached a sitting position. The room swam, but she battled the dizziness and focused on the detective again. "Not to be rude, but how good is your best?"

"That's not rude at all. In fact, I get asked that question all the time." She sounded pleasant enough, but Rachael heard frustration in her voice. "I've been a deputy for twelve years and a detective for the last seven of them. My case closure rate is the highest on our team."

"I'm confused," Rachael said. "Are you a detective or a deputy?"

"Both, actually. All sworn staff except the sheriff himself are deputies, no matter the rank or position attained in the agency. So, for example, Jake is a sergeant in charge of the First Response Squad, but he's still a deputy."

"First Response Squad. That's the team who came to my rescue."

Jake nodded. "We're a team of six and are dispatched on emergency callouts, especially those with a potential hostage situation."

"Please thank the others on the team for me," she said.

He nodded. "Detective Hunter serves as a negotiator on the team, but she is a well-qualified detective, too."

For some reason Rachael trusted his opinion. "Okay, good. Then let's get those questions out of the way. I want to visit Pam and Kelly, and I need to talk to my staff at the center and call all of my parents."

"Slow down there." The detective held up her hands. "Ms. Baldwin is off limits until I take her statement, and we can't allow you to talk to her."

Rachael met her gaze. "Why in the world not?"

"When people involved in incidents compare stories, they often alter their own stories to match."

"I wouldn't do that."

"It's not a conscious thing," Jake offered. "But it happens."

"Okay, fine. I'll wait to talk to Pam, but I can still get my records from the center to call the parents and my staff."

"In this age of technology, I'm surprised you don't keep that information on your phone," Jake said.

"Some directors may, but I don't. I care for a hundred and twenty children, and I won't risk having my phone stolen and the contact information for these families falling into the wrong hands. Besides that, for tax purposes, I keep my business and work activities separate whenever possible. I do keep the contact information on an iPad that I take home every day and use for center business only. Since I came by ambulance from the center, my iPad is still in my office."

"I'm sorry, but you won't be able to go to the center," the detective said. "It's a crime scene. Only official personnel are allowed inside, and it will remain closed during the initial investigation."

"Closed?" Rachael asked. "For how long?"

"We won't know for sure. I can give you a better estimate later in the day."

"Then it's even more important for me to get going and find a way to contact the parents. Many of them are low-income and can't afford to miss even a day of work, and I need to help them find alternative care. I also have to notify my state licensing representative, who will need to complete her own investigation." Rachael swung her legs over the edge of the bed and nearly tumbled to the floor.

Jake grabbed her arm to steady her. Warmth from his touch rushed up her arm. Shocked at her response, she pulled her arm free.

He met her gaze and held it. "It's admirable to want to take care of these people, but it's not wise to leave before the doctor releases you."

"He's already given the okay. I'm just waiting for the nurse to take out my IV and bring my papers." She raised her chin to show her sincerity in helping her families. "The parents must be frantic over what's happened. Can't I at least pick up my iPad so I can call them?"

Jake turned to his fellow deputy. "What if, after Ms. Long answers your questions, I accompany her to the center and keep an eye on her while she gathers any information she needs?"

Detective Hunter arched a brow, watching Jake like a hawk. She didn't look happy with him. "I'll have to check with our forensic team, but if they've processed the office, then that should be fine."

He turned his focus back to Rachael. "Our questions won't take long."

The detective leaned against the wall, appearing casual and at ease, but her eyes were sharp and direct. "You seem especially fond of Kelly. Do you have a connection to her other than as the center director?"

"Connection?" Rachael thought about it as she planted her feet on the floor to test her strength. "I'm fond of all the children at the center. In fact, I take care of some of them at my house when their parents have to work outside the normal center hours. I guess I care for Kelly more often than most, so I might be a bit more protective of her."

Detective Hunter flashed a knowing look at Jake, who gave an almost imperceptible shrug.

"But today you chose to watch Kelly at the center," the detective said.

"It just made more sense to have Pam bring Kelly to the center as they live nearby. She'd have to take several buses to get to my house. Plus Pam would have dropped Kelly at my house right when I'd have to leave to open the center."

"Why don't you tell us what happened this morning," he said. "Every detail."

Rachael would rather not have to rehash all of the details, but she had to do everything she could to make sure they caught this creep. "The day started out crazy. Pam has been late for work a few times because we don't open until six thirty. So this week, I've been opening at six so she can get to work on time. I should mention that my center is licensed by the state, and I am required to operate within my posted hours. So by opening at six, I violated my licensing agreement."

"And yet you did so," Skyler said.

"Yes, for Pam," Rachael said. "But you should also know if the schedule needed to continue beyond this week, I would have called my licensing rep and asked to change my hours. Also when my teacher was late and Pam needed to get to work, I should have made Pam wait, as licensing regulations require two staff members be on-site when children are present."

Rachael paused and looked away. "You must think I'm a terrible person, but I strive to follow the rules, and I realize I made a mistake. It's not an excuse, but I did it for Pam and Kelly. If Pam lost her job, she would have to apply for government subsidies and that could be endangered by her past drug use. She's afraid she would lose custody of Kelly. That wouldn't be good for either of them."

"What will happen when licensing learns of your actions?" Jake asked.

"I don't know. Since I've never had a violation before, I hope they'll give me the benefit of the doubt."

"Let's hope so," Jake said.

"So you took Kelly," Skyler said, moving them back to the incident.

"Since she was sleeping, Pam laid her in the crib, and then she went to work." At the thought of precious Kelly lying there oblivious to the masked man, Rachael's voice caught, but she forced down the anguish, just as she did whenever she thought of the child she'd lost in a miscarriage.

Detective Hunter raised an eyebrow. "I don't pretend to know anything about child care centers, but it seems odd to me that even if one teacher was late, there weren't other teachers present."

"That's typical for us. Staffing is the largest expense in child care, and very few children arrive when the center opens. To save on staffing dollars we combine all age groups when we open, and ramp up the staffing as the morning progresses. My next teacher was due in at seven."

"I'll need to see your time cards to confirm this is the norm."

Rachael couldn't imagine why the detective had to confirm that, but she had nothing to hide. "I can get them for you once I'm allowed back in the center."

The detective jotted down a few notes on a small notepad, then looked up. "So, you were alone in the room with Kelly. What happened next?"

"I was putting fresh sheets on the other mattresses when a masked man pried the door open and pointed a gun at me."

"I noticed you have an alarm system at the center. Didn't this set off an alarm?"

She shook her head. "During times when children are present, we turn off the burglar alarm for the building. The front door remains locked for safety reasons. During open hours, each parent has a code to enter on a keypad to gain access through the front door."

"This keypad is only at the main entrance?"

"That's right. When I arrive, the first thing I do is turn off the burglar alarm, and then, when I'm ready to open, I activate the parent controls at the front door."

"Okay, the man is in the baby room and holding a

gun on you," the detective continued. "What does he do next?"

"He told me he was going to take Kelly, and he threatened to hurt me if I didn't cooperate. I tried to protect her, but he overpowered me. He gave me that shot, and I fought him off. I don't know what happened after the drug took effect."

"You fought hard," Jake added. "You should be proud of the way you stood up for Kelly."

Her ribs ached from the man's grip, and her arms were bruised from trying to escape, but only she and the intruder could possibly know that he had manhandled her.

She eyed Jake. "How do you know what happened?"

"We accessed your center's closed-circuit video."

"Oh, right. The video. I should have thought of that."

"You have quite a system." An accusation of some sort lingered in the detective's tone.

"I installed it for parents to be able to check on their children any time of the day. They can all log in to view a live feed." She shook her head. "Thankfully there wasn't a reason for any of them to watch this morning."

Jake pulled a chair up to her bed. A hint of his musky aftershave drifted over, and she peered at him. This close, she could see striations of black and gold in his eyes, and she couldn't pull her gaze free.

"Forget I'm a deputy," he said softly. "I'm just Jake. The guy who held your hand in the ambulance. I'm sorry we have to question you after all you've been through. It's just routine. We'll make this as quick and painless as possible. Then I'll give you a ride to your center."

Detective Hunter pointedly cleared her throat.

Rachael suspected Jake was breaking the rules of questioning, or maybe he didn't care about the rules but truly wanted to help her through a difficult time. Either way, the detective didn't seem to like it.

"We were unable to see the intruder's face on the video," he continued. "But I know you ripped off his mask. Can you describe him?"

"Other than getting to see Kelly and Pam and talking to my center families, I've thought of little else, but I can only call up a vague image of his face. It's too fuzzy to see in detail. I do remember his eyes though...his eyes and his breath."

"Go on," Jake encouraged her.

"His eyes were mean and hard. Like he enjoyed hurting us. They were gray, almost black. His breath was minty fresh, like a man who takes good care of himself." She paused to calm her nerves. "I know it's a weird thing to remember, but I didn't expect a kidnapper to have good hygiene."

Detective Hunter pushed off the wall and stepped forward. "Since you're the only one who can identify him, I need you to keep trying to picture his face."

"What about one of the neighbors?" Rachael asked. "Or someone on the street, or the person who called 911? Maybe they saw him before he put on his mask."

"Deputies are canvassing the neighborhood right now, but the woman who called this in didn't see his face."

"Go back earlier in your day," Jake said, changing the subject. "On your way to work, or even in the last few days, did you notice anything out of the ordinary?"

"Like I said, I expected to see my teacher waiting for me in the parking lot, but she wasn't there. She called to tell me she had a flat tire and had to take the bus." Guilt crowded out other thoughts, and Rachael bit down on her lip.

"What is it?" Jake asked.

"If I'd waited for her to get there before letting Pam go, maybe this wouldn't have happened."

"If an armed man wanted Kelly," Jake said, "he would've taken her even with two people present, and something bad could have happened to Ms. Baldwin or your teacher."

"Unless, of course, Ms. Baldwin is involved in this somehow," Detective Hunter said.

"Pam? Involved? But why? She has full custody of Kelly. She has no need to kidnap her."

"You mentioned that she had a past drug problem. Maybe she started using again and needed money," the detective said bluntly.

"No." Rachael shook her head hard. The room spun, so she waited for it to still before continuing. "Pam is clean, and if you think she'd fake a kidnapping to sell Kelly to someone, you're wrong. Pam loves Kelly, and she's a good mother. She'd never hurt her child."

The detective fixed her eyes on Rachael. "What about you?"

Rachael swiveled to face her directly. The room swam, but she grabbed the arm of Jake's chair. "You think I'm involved in Kelly's attempted kidnapping? That's unbelievable. I would never do that. Never. Not in a million years."

Jake stood. "I think this is enough for now."

Rachael shot him a look. "You think I did this, too?"

"I—" Jake said, but the door opened and the nurse entered, taking his attention.

She didn't seem to notice the tension in the room, but smiled and marched across the small space. "Let's take that IV out so you can get going." The nurse cocked an eyebrow at Jake and the detective. "If you'll excuse us…"

"I'll wait in the hall to give you a ride to the center," Jake said.

Rachael nodded, but she wasn't sure if she should be glad for his help or concerned about spending more time with him. Especially if he thought her capable of kidnapping an innocent little baby.

THREE

Jake hated leaving Rachael behind, but he stepped into the hallway anyway, the Christmas music playing overhead barely registering as Rachael lingered in his thoughts.

Skyler followed him from the room, grabbed his sleeve and pulled him out of the bustle of hospital staff scurrying down the hallway. They must have made a sight, the small, slender woman dragging him across the hall. People often took one glance at her stature and girl-next-door look, and then underestimated her skills as a law enforcement officer.

She planted her hands on her hips and glared up at him. "What're you doing? You want to sabotage this case before it begins?"

He'd expected her to pounce the minute they'd entered the hallway. She was fierce at her job and worked tirelessly to close her cases. He owed it to her to do a better job of containing his feelings and not getting in her way.

Still, he would voice his opinion. "I told you before. I'm not liking Rachael for this."

"I'll ignore the fact that you're choosing to call her Rachael instead of Ms. Long, but physically holding her hand? That's going a little far, isn't it?" Skyler sharpened her gaze, and he felt like a suspect under her watchful eye in an interrogation room.

"She was worried, and I helped her through it," Jake said to downplay his role that had gone beyond professional.

Law enforcement officers held victims' hands all the time, but he knew in his heart that he didn't take her hand for that reason. They had a connection and he wanted to offer her comfort.

His need to protect her had hit him the minute he'd seen her on the video when she'd bravely stood in front of a gunman, risking her life for a helpless baby. It took a strong woman to stand up to such a threat, and yet, at that moment and even later, he'd seen an extreme vulnerability in her eyes. He wanted to do whatever it took to help her.

Maybe when the medic asked if they could call anyone for her, and Jake had learned that she had no one, he'd wanted to make sure she had support. Or maybe he'd transferred his thing for protecting kids onto her. But as a law enforcement officer, especially a supervisor who should set an example for others, he had to step back, put up a professional wall and not let her distress get to him.

And, of course, Skyler picked up on that.

"You better make sure that's all it is," she continued. "Because despite what we think about Ms. Long, she has to remain a suspect. Especially since she admitted to a special bond with Kelly, and she often takes care of her. Maybe she thinks since her husband died, she'll never have a child of her own. Maybe she thinks she'd be a better mother than Ms. Baldwin, that she'd be doing Kelly a favor by taking her."

"If that's the case, she wouldn't go about it in such

a violent way, and she certainly wouldn't risk being drugged."

"Maybe not, but unless you stop with the whole protective thing and allow me to question her thoroughly, we won't get anywhere in this case."

"Did you consider the fact that as a child care director, she couldn't possibly have a sketchy past? Not with the way child care workers are vetted in Oregon."

"Be that as it may, I need to do a thorough job, and you're getting in my way of finding this creep." The color in her face drained away, and she looked like she might be ill.

"Are you okay?"

She grabbed the wall and took long breaths as she ran a hand over her face. "I'm fine, and let's not change the subject. I need your help, Jake. Not your interference."

Jake leveled his gaze on her. "When the nurse is finished, we'll talk to Rachael again."

"No, *I'll* talk to her." Skyler raised her shoulders, which she often did to make herself seem bigger, but one hand lingered on the wall. "You may be my supervisor on the team, but you have no say in my detective duties, and you'll stay out here."

Jake smiled wryly at Skyler putting him in his place. "I'll come with you, but you can do all the talking."

"It's best if I go in alone."

He knew he should stand down. Take off. Leave Rachael behind as he did with victims on all other callouts, but he couldn't make his feet head in the opposite direction. He could temper his actions, though, and move closer to toeing the official line.

"Tell you what," he said. "I'll find out where Rachael keeps her iPad, and then, while you question her, I'll head over to the center to pick it up so she can make her calls.

When you're finished, I'll escort her home and stay with her until we can assign a protection detail."

Skyler's gaze didn't lighten up. "I know the kidnapper said he would kill her, but do you think he'll keep coming after her?"

"It didn't sound like an idle threat. As long as we aren't showing up at his door to arrest him, he has to know we haven't identified him, giving him a chance to stop her from doing so now or accusing him in a trial."

"You're right. She needs protection."

He held out his hand. "Then we have a deal?"

"Deal." She sounded reluctant but shook his hand.

"Let me just tell Rachael about the change in plans, and she's all yours."

As they stepped to the door, Skyler's phone rang. "I need to take this, but I'll make it quick."

He pushed through the door and found Rachael lying back on the bed, her eyes closed. He studied her face, the high cheekbones and long eyelashes lying on them. Her face hadn't regained much color, and her breathing still seemed shallow. He wished she would wake up so he could get a read on how well she was coping before Skyler came into the room.

The wish mimicked the one he'd made at the US embassy in Nairobi. A wish for his parents and his younger sister and brother.

Even in twenty-plus years, the incident hadn't faded from his memory. He could still hear the earth-rending explosion, feel the ground rumbling under his feet and taste the dust filling the air. He'd been only thirteen, but in that instant, he knew his family was in trouble. He'd charged down the road only to learn the rubble trapped his family, and he could do nothing to help. He hadn't been there when they'd needed him, and the bomb ensured they wouldn't ever wake up again.

If he'd been at the embassy instead of slipping out to hang with friends his parents didn't approve of, he could have helped. Sure, he was only a teenager, but he lived every day with the certainty that he could have done something to save their lives. At the funeral, he'd promised his parents that he'd make up for not being there for them, and he'd devoted his life to helping others in need.

An ache in his chest caught his attention. The deputy-inflicted bullets bruised his flesh, but the loss of his family overtook the pain. He'd managed to keep the familiar ache at bay for many years. Today, though, the sting raked through his body as intensely as the day they'd died.

"Why you, Rachael Long?" he whispered. "Why, after all these years, are you bringing out feelings I thought were long gone?"

"Did you say something?" Skyler asked, stepping up behind him.

"No!" Rachael suddenly cried out and jerked awake. Terror darkened her eyes as she shot a panicked look around the room. She'd probably relived the kidnapping attempt in her sleep.

Jake knew all about bad dreams. The bomb had rumbled through his sleep for years. He wanted to take her hand, but after his talk with Skyler, he shoved both of them in his pockets instead. At that moment, he hated his job.

Rachael would remain on Skyler's suspect list, and after he'd gone, she'd question Rachael until she felt confident she'd gotten complete answers. Then she'd tear into Rachael's background, dig deep and ferret out any secrets or past indiscretions that hinted at her involvement. Many of those would then be reviewed with Rachael so she could offer an explanation.

Not that Skyler would focus solely on Rachael. As a good detective, she would look for other leads and keep Rachael's role in perspective. He could count on Skyler to be impartial, but he didn't care about the other suspects at this point.

Rachael remained his focus. His only focus right now.

Sitting in a wheelchair held firmly by a hospital staff member, Rachael gazed out the window to avoid the odd looks cast her way by people stepping through the lobby entrance. Detective Hunter had ordered Rachael to surrender her clothing for the forensic staff to process in hopes of finding the intruder's DNA. The hospital had given her two gowns to wear back-to-back to cover herself, and a lightweight robe for warmth. Though fully covered, she was essentially wearing pajamas in public.

"Joy to the World" played on the speakers above, and the woman holding on to her chair hummed along in a sharp pitch. If that wasn't enough to remind Rachael Christmas was just a week away, large trees trimmed in reds and golds perfumed the air with a thick pine scent, and snow that was unusual for Portland dusted the ground outside.

A battered white truck pulled into the patient pickup area, and Jake jumped down from the vehicle. Before he'd left her hospital room, he'd told her he would use Detective Hunter's car to go to the center for the iPad, and during that time, he would have someone retrieve his pickup from home and drop it at the hospital.

As he approached, she wanted to leap from the chair and take refuge from prying eyes inside his truck, but the bruises circling her body ensured she wouldn't be leaping in her near future.

He opened the passenger door and gazed down on her, his tender expression one she'd seen several times today. He offered his hand—another kind gesture from this man she found so intriguing.

After what happened the last time they'd touched, she didn't want any physical contact, but dizziness continued to plague her, and she also didn't want to do a face-plant in the snow. And if she stumbled, the hospital employee might drag her back inside for another examination. Rachael wouldn't stay at the hospital any longer. Not for any reason.

She placed her hand in his, letting the long fingers wrap around hers and gently move her into the pickup that looked like it had seen better days. She willed her mind not to dwell on the warmth and strength of his hand and to pay attention to getting into the truck without hitting the concrete.

Once she settled back, Jake started to close the door, but she stopped him and leaned out.

"Thank you," she called to the woman who'd wheeled her outside.

"Yes, thank you," Jake added and closed the door with a solid thump.

He said something else to the transport woman that elicited a broad smile on her chubby face. Maybe he was just a big flirt, and this connection between them was a common occurrence in his life. Even more reason to ignore her unwanted interest in him.

When he settled behind the wheel, his presence seemed to take up the entire space, and she wedged herself closer to the door, tugging her robe tighter around her. He'd set the heat on high, and the air rushing from the vents warmed her bare legs.

As he pointed the truck down the driveway, a hand-beaded ornament swung from his rearview mirror. The delicate star boasting golden points and a bright blue interior seemed in direct contrast to his tough exterior and the manly truck. Obviously a vintage item, she suspected he had a story behind the ornament, and she didn't know what to make of it, of him. He was such an enigma. One minute kind and protective, the next all business. She hadn't a clue which guy was the real Jake Marsh.

It didn't much matter, though. Even if he'd struck some cord in her that had been dormant since Eli died, she'd fight the feelings. She would never expose herself to the searing loss that opening her heart again could bring.

Trouble was, when Jake had first taken the chair across from her and looked into her eyes, she'd seen something that resonated deep inside, like maybe he understood the pain and guilt that plagued her. Like maybe he would understand if she mentioned that after her husband died, grief consumed her and she hadn't properly cared for herself. When she reached her fifth month of pregnancy, she'd miscarried. Maybe he'd even hold her and try to convince her that she shouldn't blame herself.

Right, and people had wings and could fly, too.

Point-blank, her husband and child were gone, and this man could do nothing to assuage her guilt. After all, God hadn't been able to erase it, so why would she think a man could?

She'd learned that nothing good came from brooding over the past, so she trained her gaze out the window until they turned onto her street.

"Almost there," he said.

A sigh slipped out before she could stop it.

"If this is about all the questions we had to ask," he said, "I'm sorry, but you fit the profile for an infant abductor."

Surprised at his announcement, she swiveled. "What exactly is that profile?"

"Female. In your childbearing years. Same race as the child abducted. An overwhelming loss in your past. Your husband, I mean."

"A zillion other women fit that description, too," she responded, thinking it was only a matter of time before they learned of her miscarriage. Then her suspect potential would grow exponentially.

"But these other women didn't have access to Kelly, nor were they her caregiver."

She crossed her arms. "I'm not the only woman who has access to Kelly. Besides, what do you think I would do with her if I arranged the kidnapping? It's not like I can show up to work holding a baby that everyone would recognize."

"But you could close down the center and move out of town."

"I'd never close my center. These parents need the service I provide, and it's my way of…" She wouldn't tell him her service helped her atone for her role in Eli's and the baby's deaths. "Never mind. If Detective Hunter keeps digging into my life, she'll soon know I'm not behind this."

He eyed her for a moment. "What about parents or staff members who might have recently lost a child? Like a miscarriage or a child dying. Has that happened to any of them?"

He'd clearly described her, sending her heart plummeting. "Why is that a concern?"

"Losing a child is one of the biggest reasons women abduct other children."

So she'd been right on track thinking if she admitted her own miscarriage, that, along with the other items he mentioned earlier, would move her from suspect to prime suspect. Then the investigative focus would fall solely on her, which would not help them find the kidnapper.

"None of my staff or parents have lost a child," she said without elaborating.

He nodded. "Then we'll expand beyond the center to other people in Pam Baldwin's life. Do you know if she has friends or any female family members who might fit this description?"

"In an effort to stay clean, she left all the people she did drugs with in the past, and I don't think she's had the time to make new friends. I suppose one of her coworkers could have lost a child. All I know about her family is that she's not close to her parents."

"Does she have a boyfriend?"

Rachael shook her head. "Not that I know of."

"Okay, then our focus will likely remain on you and your staff members for the time being."

"My staff members?"

He nodded. "They have access to Kelly, so Detective Hunter will be interviewing them, and they'll remain under suspicion until we can rule them out."

Great. Now they were going to grill her teachers, too. All of the caring, compassionate women who'd worked beside her for three years. Women who'd no sooner hurt Kelly than she would.

"They didn't do this," she said. "Pick on me all you want, but please don't harass them."

"We're harassing you? Is that what you think?"

"What else can I think? I was attacked this morning,

which should prove my innocence, but you don't seem to care." Her voice wobbled, and she hated that she came across as weak and whiny.

He slowed at a stop sign and fixed a steady gaze on her. "I care, Rachael, but our mission is to find this guy as quickly as possible before he hurts anyone else. If that means we have to keep you on our suspect list no matter what we think about your innocence, then that's what we'll do."

She studied him carefully, looking for any hint of his real opinion of her. "So you don't think I'm involved?"

He turned back to his driving and didn't answer, which, she supposed, was an answer in itself and the end to their conversation. She peered out the window. The clouds had broken, and one of Oregon's famous rainbows hung in the sky, the muted colors giving her hope that God had something good planned for her future.

She recommitted herself to staying strong, not for herself, but for the center's parents and staff. She used her pain to make a difference in others' lives, and that had been the only thing that had taken her out of her grief and allowed her to live again. She just needed to keep that in mind and be thankful for her opportunities.

She closed her eyes.

Thank you, Lord, for keeping Kelly safe. For Jake and his team. Continue to watch over her. Over all of us. And help them find the intruder.

She kept her eyes closed until she felt the car bump into the driveway of the house she'd purchased when she'd opened the center. Living in the home she and Eli had shared had been too painful, and when God finally showed her how to move on in life, she knew she couldn't continue to live in the home that held so many memories.

"Deputy Keith Hill." Jake nodded at the patrol car sitting in front of her bungalow. "He's got this shift."

"Thanks again for arranging for his protection. I feel much safer."

Jake reached behind the seat and lifted out her iPad. "I found it in the drawer right where you said it would be."

He handed it to her, and she clutched it to her chest like a lifeline. She might not be allowed back into the center where she'd pinned all of her hopes and dreams the last few years, but she had her connection to the families through this device.

He reached behind the seat again. "I also grabbed your purse. I figured you'd need keys and such."

"Right, my keys. I didn't even think of that." She smiled at him. "Thank you."

He gave a quick, almost uncomfortable nod as though he didn't like to have any attention drawn to his helpfulness. He'd acted the same way when she'd thanked him at the hospital, claiming his team had done all the work.

"We should get you inside." He opened his door, the hinge groaning in protest. His vehicle had to be ten-plus years old, and it looked well used. Still, it seemed like the kind of vehicle he would own. Something serviceable, but not showy or pretentious.

After he came around the front of the truck, he opened her door and offered his hand again. She accepted his help, and once she'd found solid footing, his hand moved to the small of her back and urged her toward the home she'd painted a crisp white with blue trim.

She fished out her keys and unlocked the bright blue door, pushing it open before turning to bid Jake goodbye.

She suddenly wished he didn't have to leave, and at the same time hoped he would. "Thank you for the ride. For everything, actually."

"I'd like to have a look around your house just to be safe."

Her heart fluttered. "You don't think the intruder has come here, do you?"

"I doubt it," he said, sounding sure of his opinion. "But I don't want to take any chances."

"I don't, either." Though she didn't like the thought of being alone with him when she was emotional and vulnerable to his kindness, she stepped back.

"I'll make it quick." He brushed past her, and his sure steps took him straight into her house.

She closed and locked the door, then trailed him as he went through the main living areas of her house. At the back door, he rested his hand on his weapon, and it remained in place as he peered out the kitchen window into her backyard.

He spun. "If you'll give me the key, I'll check your garage."

She lifted a key from a peg on the wall and handed it to him.

"It's not a good idea to keep your keys hanging in plain sight," he said. "There are bad people in this world. You experienced that today, and you don't want to make things easier for them. If someone did break into your house, they'd have keys to your car and any other keys you keep hanging here." He didn't wait for a response from her but stepped out the door. She watched him cross her small backyard to the single-car garage.

She'd never really given a lot of thought to personal safety. At least not beyond knowing full well that people died in car crashes and that she should be extra-vigilant while driving, plus avoiding dangerous situations. She paid attention to her surroundings, but such things were probably on Jake's mind most of the time.

How difficult it would be to live under those terms. She wished no one had to be constantly on guard. She was even more thankful for men and women like Jake and his team, who dedicated their lives to protecting people.

He secured the garage door, and when he returned, he put the keys in her hand instead of hanging them on the peg.

They toured the remainder of the house where he paid special attention to the closets and the space under the beds. She appreciated his thoroughness but hoped he didn't find too many dust bunnies.

Back at the front door, he reached into his pocket and pulled out a business card. "My cell is on here. Call me if you need anything. No matter what. No matter the time." He kept his gaze glued to hers and looked torn about leaving, but stepped outside.

At the stairs, he paused to look back. His gaze connected with hers and held. He hid his emotions, but she could tell he wanted to stay.

"Thank you for everything," she said to get him moving.

He gave a sharp nod then jogged down to the sidewalk. She watched him climb into his truck and back out of the driveway before she closed and locked the door. She set her purse on the hall table and added her iPad, too. The center parents and staff needed to hear from her, but she simply had to change out of the hospital gowns and shower off the creepy-crawly feeling from the intruder's touch.

In her bathroom, she gingerly removed the gowns and looked at her stomach in the mirror. Two-inch-wide bruises already circled her body, the deep purple attesting to her struggle against the intruder's iron grip. No wonder her pain had continued to grow after the ketamine had worn off.

She turned on the shower, cranked the knob to steaming hot and climbed under the spray. The water cascaded over her back and circled the drain. She grabbed a bar of soap. The slippery slice shot from her hands and pinged around the tile walls until it landed at her feet. Bending to retrieve it, dizziness assaulted her again. She planted her hands on her knees and held her position to let it clear. Thankfully, most of the drug had left her system and she could function, but she wished it would dissipate even faster.

Maybe then she wouldn't be so emotional and weepy around Detective Hunter and Jake. She just couldn't imagine that either of them truly believed she had participated in Kelly's attempted kidnapping. Waking up at the center came to mind, the sight of Jake's caring face, his smile and concern. Then he'd held Kelly out so she could see the baby was fine. Joy had nearly burst her heart and she'd thought him to be an ally.

And now?

Until the detective proved Rachael had no part in the attempted kidnapping, she would be alone in her defense—much like she was alone in life. For the first time since she'd come to grips with losing Eli and the baby, the loneliness nearly bothered her more than she could bear.

Tears threatened again, burning at the back of her eyes for release.

No. She wouldn't let them take over. She didn't want to be stuffed up for her phone calls. She could let herself cry after her families were taken care of.

She slowly stood and grabbed a washcloth to scrub the horrible attack from her body. As the cloth ran over her skin, she imagined his touch sliding away. By the time she finished and dressed in yoga pants and a sweatshirt, the bruised areas were clean and aching even more, but she felt refreshed.

She headed to the foyer table to grab a few aspirin to take the edge off her pain.

She stepped into the family room and something red on the mirror above the fireplace caught her attention. She focused. Spotted big bold letters scribbled on the glass.

A message.

Talk and You Die.

She took a step back, clasped a hand over her mouth. He gaze shot around the room, looking for the intruder. She spotted her favorite lipstick laying open on the floor.

Terror stole her breath. Her throat closed down as if hands had come around her neck and squeezed.

She took another step back. Then another. And another.

She was aware of screams coming from somewhere.

They had to be from her, but she could barely breathe. How could she be the one screaming?

FOUR

Hair-raising screams greeted Jake when he parked in Rachael's driveway and opened his car door. Deputy Hill was already out of his car and jogging toward her house, his gun drawn.

Jake drew his service weapon as adrenaline raced through his veins.

Thankfully, he'd come back. He'd traveled a short distance but couldn't forget the forlorn look on Rachael's face as he departed, so he'd turned around. Looked like he'd done so just in time.

He charged across the lawn to step in front of Hill.

"Update me," Jake demanded as he marched toward the entrance.

"No movement near the house," Hill said. "The woman just started screaming from inside."

Jake shot a look around the yard. "You're sure you didn't just miss someone?"

"Positive. I didn't take my eyes off the property."

Jake knew nothing about Deputy Hill, so there was no telling if he'd actually been as attentive as he claimed, but if his tone of voice was any indication, he was telling the truth.

Staying aware of his surroundings, Jake climbed the steps. At the door, he took a quick look through the window. He could see through the foyer, and he spotted Rachael standing in the living room, but he couldn't tell if she was alone. Her arms were wrapped around her waist, her head thrown back, but her wailing screams were subsiding.

He had to get into the house, but he couldn't endanger her more by racing inside without knowing if she was alone. If someone was with her, Jake could force a hostage situation and that was the last thing he wanted.

He turned the knob and tugged. It didn't budge.

Rachael must have heard him, as she suddenly spun around and peered at him for a long moment. Then, like a zombie, she strolled toward the door and her trembling hands hovered over the lock before she turned it. Not saying a word, she stood back. Terror filled her eyes.

He stepped into the foyer and moved her between him and Deputy Hill for her safety. "What is it?"

She lifted an arm and pointed into the living room.

"He...he was...he was here." The words came out in a strangled whisper.

He had to assume she was talking about the intruder.

"Wait here," he told her and glanced at Hill. "Back me up."

Together they eased forward, Jake's gaze traveling every inch of the space in search of a threat. At the wide doorway to the living room, he glanced back to be sure Rachael was okay. She remained frozen in place, so he ran his gaze over the living room. He saw a message written on the mirror above the fireplace.

Talk and You Die.

If the kidnapper left the message, he meant that if she told anyone she'd seen him he would kill her. She was right. The intruder *had* come here.

Jake finished his visual search of the room to confirm no threat existed, and spotted a lipstick lying on the floor.

"You think the mirror's the thing that scared her?" Hill asked from behind. "I mean, even I'd be a little freaked out if I found a message of any kind written on my mirror, but one that said, 'Talk and You Die'? That'd freak me out big-time."

Jake wouldn't admit his fear when they had a job to do. "The suspect could still be in the house, and we can't let Ms. Long out of our sight. You stay with her while I clear the rest of the house again."

Jake took his job seriously, and the first rule of law enforcement was to protect life at all costs, so he waited for Hill to return to Rachael.

"Stay alert," Jake warned, his gaze connecting with her eyes. He acknowledged her with a quick nod, then turned his attention back to the house and moved through the rooms ending up in the kitchen. The door leading to the yard stood wide open. He checked the door and the frame. He wasn't surprised to see pry marks, raising his unease.

Jake continued onto the small back porch, then searched the postage-stamp-sized yard and her garage again. Certain the intruder was gone, he grabbed his phone and dialed Skyler. He told her of the break-in and why he thought it had been the kidnapper who'd left the message.

"I need forensics here ASAP," he said.

"You're sure Rachael didn't write this message herself to draw us off track?"

He didn't take any offense at Skyler's question, as it was a logical one, and she wasn't here to see Rachael's abject terror declaring her innocence. "I'm sure. The back door has been jimmied."

"Our resources are already spread thin today." Skyler

sighed. "But I'll get someone out as soon as I can. I'll likely have to pull someone off the center to cover it."

The county had limited forensic resources, and he hated that processing Rachael's house would slow them down, but it couldn't be helped.

"How soon before you'll get here?" he asked.

"I'm at the center and can be there in five."

He wanted to ask if she'd located anything new in her investigation, but he could do that when she arrived, and Rachael needed his attention. He disconnected his call and stepped back into the kitchen, taking the time to look around as he grabbed a glass from an open shelf and filled it with water for Rachael. The bright space had white cabinets and a light swirly granite countertop. Red stools sat at a big island, and she'd also included red items throughout.

Back in the living room, he ran his gaze over the space, looking for any lead he might have missed. Beyond the message, what he noticed most was the absence of Christmas, which was just a week away. His gaze moved to the message that was written in the plum-colored lipstick lying on the floor. The letters were sloppy and hastily scribbled.

A worn wood fireplace mantel was mounted below the mirror and held a picture of Rachael and a man looking very much in love. Her deceased husband, Jake suspected. The room was immaculate and spotless, just like the kitchen, but besides the frame there weren't any personal touches in the room, making the house feel sterile and cold. It was the opposite of his first impression of Rachael.

Intrigued even more, he joined her in the entryway. She was sitting in a chair in the corner, chewing on a fingernail. She looked up, terror still lingering in her expression. He gave her the glass. She cupped it between both hands but didn't take a drink.

Jake faced Hill. "The house is clear. I found the back door open."

"He came through the alley, then," Hill said, sounding relieved that he hadn't missed seeing the kidnapper. "You need me for anything here, or can I go out to my vehicle and check in with dispatch?"

"Go," Jake replied, then turned his attention to Rachael.

"He was in here, wasn't he?" she asked.

"Yes," Jake said as calmly as possible when all he wanted to do was slam a fist against the wall.

"I was in the shower, and he was out here prowling around my house." She shuddered.

Anger burned in his gut at the intruder for causing her fear, but it wouldn't help to let his anger show. Remaining calm and moving forward was the best way to help her deal with her emotions. "I'm assuming he used your lipstick to write the message?"

She looked up and pointed at her handbag sitting on the entry table. "It was in my purse."

At the look of utter violation on her face, he wanted to take her hand, but after Skyler's comments, he ignored his instinct in favor of keeping things professional. "Once our forensic staff processes your house, I'll need you to make a thorough inspection to see if anything has been disturbed or is missing."

She nodded, but it was wooden.

"Is there anyone I can call for you?"

In the ambulance, she'd said she had no one, but he hoped she had a close friend who could come over and help her handle this latest shock.

"Anyone?" She stared blankly ahead. "No. There's no one to call."

He'd been saddened by her attacks and wanted to help her, but now he felt a need to stay by her side.

"After my husband died, I was in a bad way for a long time," she said quietly. "When I finally figured out that I had to move on, I also realized I couldn't live in the same house, and I bought this place. It's been a haven to me, but now..." She looked up at him, her eyes watery.

Skyler's demands aside, he couldn't stand by and do nothing. He squatted next to Rachael and took her hands in his. "We'll find this man. I promise. And then your home can once again be that sanctuary for you."

"Do you think it will be that simple?"

"Finding him?"

"No, going on with life as if my home hasn't been violated."

"Simple? No. But people do it all the time, and I get the sense that you're not one to let circumstances get you down."

"I did. When Eli died and the..." She shook her head. "But you're right. That loss challenged me to the extreme, and if I can come through that, I can come through anything."

He noted a hint of resolve in her voice, so he let go of her hands and sat back on his heels. "I suspect you haven't gotten to those calls you need to make."

"No."

"Perhaps now would be a good time to do that. It will give you something to occupy your mind while the forensic staff does their thing."

"Okay."

"They'll be working in all areas of your house, so if

you'd like privacy for the calls, I suggest you move out to my truck."

"My cell phone is still at the center, so can I use yours to make the calls?"

"Sure."

She got up. "Can I get a jacket from the closet?"

He nodded, and she retrieved a red wool coat, then picked up her iPad from the table. He escorted her to the truck. Skyler was just pulling up to the curb.

He handed his keys to Rachael. "I'll be inside with Detective Hunter. Feel free to run the heater if you get cold."

He closed the door and went to meet Skyler. She took a long look at Rachael, then met his gaze.

"She's making her calls to the parents," he explained. "I thought she'd like privacy, and she can't move around the house until forensics is finished."

Skyler nodded. "Show me what we've got."

Jake led the way to the porch, where Skyler dropped a box of booties by the door and gave a pair to Jake so they didn't accidentally track substances onto the scene and confuse the evidence. She slipped on a pair herself. Without a word, he led her to the living room mirror.

She studied the writing from all angles and took several pictures. "Did you ask Ms. Long if this is her lipstick?"

"She kept it in her purse. She left her purse on the entryway table when she came home and then went straight to the shower."

"It had to freak her out that the guy broke in while she was showering."

Jake suspected it was a female thing to feel so violated by this, and he was glad Skyler empathized with Rachael, as it might help her believe Rachael hadn't scrawled the warning.

"I have to concur with your earlier assessment. The message is clearly meant to keep Ms. Long from telling us that she saw this guy." Skyler frowned. "Show me the point of entry into the house."

Jake took her into the kitchen, and she examined the door. She squatted down and as she came to her feet, she paled as she had at the hospital and looked like she might be sick.

"You don't look so good," he said, his concern for her immediately replacing thoughts of the break-in. "Do you need to sit down?"

She shook her head, but clamped a hand on the counter and looked even queasier.

"C'mon." He took her hand and settled her on a stool at the bar. "I'll get you some water."

He crossed to the sink and filled a glass. As much as he was concerned for Skyler, he also hoped she wasn't coming down with something, because they needed her to run the investigation so they could find the would-be kidnapper.

He handed her the glass and watched her carefully to determine if she was fit for duty, or if he should send her home.

She took a small sip of water. "I got my flu shot, so I doubt it's the flu."

He rested on a stool next to her. "I can get someone else to take over."

She started to shake her head, then suddenly stopped.

He suspected the dizziness had returned. "You should go home."

She held up a hand. "I've already begun working the case. I can handle it."

"So bring me up to speed," he said, hoping it would give him time to get a true read on her condition.

She set down the glass and dug out a notepad and pen from a backpack slung over her shoulder. "I've started the background check into Pam Baldwin. She's a grocery store cashier." Skyler flipped a page in her notebook. "She arrived at work at six fifteen this morning and claims she didn't leave her register at all."

"No breaks?"

"She says no, but the manager said she took one. It would be a violation of wage and hour if she didn't get a break, and he could be covering for that. I've requested their security video to see who's telling the truth."

"And what about Kelly's father?"

"Ms. Baldwin doesn't know who the father is."

"Interesting," Jake said, letting the surprising news settle in. "Did she have a believable story for that?"

Skyler nodded. "She had a drug problem for years. Got pregnant when she was still using. She gave me the names of two guys, Sid and Hal, but she said without a DNA test there'd be no proof either of them fathered Kelly. When she found out she was pregnant, she managed to get clean and has been clean since then. She left these guys behind and has no idea where they might be hanging out these days."

Jake didn't like what he was hearing. "Please don't tell me her drug of choice was Special K."

Used as a recreational drug on the street, ketamine had other nicknames, but Special K was most commonly used.

Skyler shook her head. "Meth."

"And you're sure she's clean?"

"Can't be certain, but yeah, it's looking good. She got her current job through a prison release program. Employers enrolled in the program agree to hire people with a record for a subsidy of their wages. She's had the job since she got clean. The store no longer receives wage subsidies, but continues to do random drug testing. She's passed all of them."

"When was her last test?"

"A month ago."

"That's enough time to start using again."

Skyler set her notepad on the counter. "Maybe, but she seems like she's on the up-and-up. I talked to her coworkers and some of the staff at the child care center. They all seem to concur with my assessment."

"Rachael told me Ms. Baldwin's estranged from her parents. Do you know why?"

"The usual story of parents of an addict. She put them through the wringer and refused to give up the drugs, so they broke off all ties with her."

"But didn't she try to reconnect with them when she got clean?"

Skyler shook her head. "She didn't want them to know about Kelly. She said she was afraid they'd try to take her away from her. As far as she knows, they aren't even aware of the baby's existence."

"She could be right about them trying for custody, which would make them prime suspects for a kidnapping."

"Not if they don't know about Kelly."

"True," Jake said, a sinking feeling hitting his stomach. He'd hoped this attempted kidnapping would turn out to be a simple family custody issue that could be solved easily, but it looked like it was going to be so much more.

"I'll follow up with the grandparents to see what they have to say."

"And we need to look elsewhere, too," he said, trying to be positive. "Remember, it's possible Ms. Baldwin has hit the skids again and could be trying to sell Kelly for drug money."

"My gut just says it's not her at this point." Skyler settled back on the stool, and Jake noticed that some color had returned to her face. "If she was behind the abduction, I don't think she'd harm the director. Ms. Baldwin seems to have the utmost respect for what Ms. Long's done to help her."

"How's that?"

"Ms. Long used the money from her husband's life insurance to open the child care center. She keeps a large number of slots available for women at risk. The state pays a flat rate that doesn't meet the actual cost of care, so she subsidizes the balance of the tuition. Pam Baldwin has one of those slots."

"And you think that's enough for a potential addict to keep her cravings at bay?"

Skyler frowned at him. "All I'm saying is that if Ms. Baldwin wanted to have her daughter abducted, she wouldn't do it at the center. She gives the director great credit for helping her stay clean and productive, and Ms. Baldwin wouldn't trample all over that."

Skyler paused to take a drink of water. "You'll be happy to know Ms. Baldwin's opinion is giving me reasons to trust Ms. Long's story, as well."

"Good." Jake smiled.

"Now, don't go all soft on me. I'm not saying I'll quit investigating either one of them. That won't happen until I have proof they're telling the truth. And you should know, I'll be letting Ms. Long believe I suspect her for the kidnapping to put pressure on her. If she *is* involved, it will ideally get her to confess."

"Let's hope you rule her out long before you make her paranoid to be around you."

Skyler nodded but seemed lost in thought.

Jake wouldn't miss the opportunity to move the conversation in the direction he preferred. "So far we've been looking at the kidnapping attempt being directed at Kelly or her mother, but what if it isn't about the kidnapping per se, and was meant to hurt Rachael? Maybe someone has a beef with her, and they thought this incident would shut down the center."

"Makes sense, I suppose." Skyler tapped her pen against her notepad. "Any of the current and past parents of the center could have a grudge against Ms. Long, and I'll add them to my suspect pool."

"I imagine the teachers would be happy to tell you about parents who are or were disgruntled with Rachael or the center."

"And vice versa. I've got appointments to interview most of the staff later today. Oh, and FYI, the teacher who was scheduled to arrive at six this morning took her car in for repair. Her tires had been slashed."

"Not likely coincidental."

"No."

"So, our abductor wanted Ms. Long to be alone. Which says we have a premeditated abduction as opposed to an abduction of chance."

Skyler nodded. "We could also be dealing with someone outside the center population who has a connection to the Baldwins and lost a baby. So I'll call local obstetricians and hospitals, too."

"Good. I was going to suggest that."

The color suddenly drained from Skyler's face, and she swallowed hard.

Jake eyed her carefully. "You sure you got your flu shot?"

"Yes." She sipped the water.

"So maybe it's something else. Maybe you should get it checked out."

"I don't feel *that* sick, but if I still feel off tonight, I'll talk to Darcie."

If Skyler looked this pale tonight, she wouldn't need to ask for their team medic's help. As the mother hen of the group, Darcie would pounce the moment she laid eyes on Skyler.

"Any forensic leads at the center?" he asked.

"We lifted a short, dark hair from Ms. Long's sweater that wasn't a match to hers. It could have fallen when she ripped off the guy's mask." Skyler bent forward and rested her elbows on her knees, then hung her head.

Jake squatted down next to her. "I want you to go home. I'll get someone—"

"No! I'm going to handle this case." She took a long breath and blew it out, then repeated the action a few more times before standing. "I should get to it."

He reached out to assist her, but she stepped off before he could. In the living room, she paused and stared at the message. "You know, the thing that's bothering me about this is why this guy bothered to leave a message. If he wanted to kill Ms. Long, he had her right here in the shower. Why not do it then?"

Jake hadn't thought of that, but leaving a message didn't really make sense. "I'd like to say maybe he isn't a killer, but then he wouldn't have fired at her or Brady at the center."

"The warning could indicate Ms. Long is this guy's partner, and they're trying to throw us off the path."

"If she is partnering with him, she's the best actress I've ever seen."

Skyler eyed him. "You're an excellent judge of character, and you can read people well, so I'm tempted to say you're right, but—"

"But you can't until facts prove you out," he finished for her. "You know, when I interviewed you for the team, I liked how tenacious and gung ho you were. I've never wanted to temper it…until today." He grinned to show her he was kidding.

She laughed, and her cheeks pinked up.

The front door opened, and a female criminologist stepped inside. Rail thin, she wore white coveralls and booties over her shoes and snapped on latex gloves.

Skyler nodded at the woman then faced Jake. "I need to meet with the team."

"If you let me know when you want to take Rachael's statement and when it's clear for her to check for missing items, I'll go out and get her."

Skyler nodded and turned.

"Skyler," he said. "When we finish here, I'd like to take Rachael over to see Kelly. I think it will help her deal with everything that's happened."

Skyler turned back and eyed him. "Are you sure that's a good idea?"

"A good idea? I don't know, but someone needs to think of her best interests. As far as I can see, there's no one else in her life to do so."

In Jake's truck, Rachael tried not to think about the white-suited woman combing her house for any scrap of evidence. Or pay any attention to Jake sitting next to her with his iPad perched against the steering wheel. She had no idea what he was working on, but he'd said it had to do with the investigation. She'd completed her calls to the parents and staff. Thankfully, both the parents and her teachers seemed like they would continue to support the center. Still, she knew their loyalty depended on how long the center remained closed. Something not in her control.

Her center was licensed by Oregon's Department of Education, as were all nongovernmental child care centers in the state that served thirteen or more children. The Office of Child Care assigned a licensing representative for each center, and she needed to notify her representative of the incident and her negligence in obeying the rules.

She located her rep's number on her iPad and dialed. She picked at lint on her jacket as she listened to the phone ringing.

"Yolanda Mason," her rep answered on the fourth ring.

"It's Rachael Long. I—"

"I'm so glad you called. I left several messages on your cell phone, and I didn't think you were going to call me back."

"I'm sorry, Yolanda. My phone is in the center, and I'm not allowed back inside."

"Before we go any further, please confirm that this baby is okay."

"She's fine and with her mother."

"Good. Good. And you? Tell me what happened to you."

Rachael started at the beginning and shared the incident, but didn't add the details of her interview with Detective Hunter. And she certainly didn't bring up the message left on her mirror.

Yolanda *tsk*ed. "I'm sorry this happened to you, but you know better, now, don't you? Opening the center early and not waiting for your teacher? This is exactly why we have such protocols in the regulations."

"I know, and I'm sorry. I truly am. I was trying to help

Pam Baldwin keep her job. Her past drug abuse leaves her at risk. I didn't want her to lose her job and lose Kelly."

Yolanda remained quiet for a long time as if trying to compose her words before speaking. "You go the extra mile for all of your families, Rachael. I applaud your diligence on their behalf. And you've had a stellar reputation with our office. Well deserved, I might add, as you always followed the rules."

Maybe she would cut Rachael some slack here.

"But you took helping your parents too far." She paused again.

Rachael took a deep breath and steeled herself for bad news. They would likely put the center on a provisional license, but she deserved it.

"I'm sorry, but we're suspending your center's license," Yolanda said.

Rachael gasped.

"Suspension," she murmured, bringing Jake's gaze her way.

"I will, of course, need to conduct a full investigation," Yolanda continued. "I'd like to visit the center as soon as possible."

Tears pricked at Rachael's eyes, but she couldn't cry now. She had to remain professional so Yolanda knew she didn't fall apart at the first sign of trouble. "I can let you know when the detective in charge releases the center to me."

"And when will that be?"

"She thought they might finish today."

"In that case, I will meet you promptly at 9:00 a.m. tomorrow," she said, her tone firm. "Before then, I need you to contact your families to tell them about the suspension, and that the center is closed until further notice."

"Can this suspension be rescinded?" Rachael asked, and held her breath.

"You can appeal, but that doesn't mean it will be lifted. We can discuss the details tomorrow." She took a deep breath and blew it out over the phone. "Please, Rachael, I know you have a soft spot for all of your parents and would do just about anything to help them out, but don't be foolish and let children back into the center unless you are cleared by us to do so."

"Don't worry," Rachael said, having learned her lesson. "I won't."

She disconnected the call and stared at the phone.

"I take it that didn't go so well," Jake said.

"You have no idea," she replied and wondered if her dream of helping struggling families had just been snuffed out for good.

FIVE

The sun had sunk below the horizon before Rachael finished checking her home, allowing Jake to drive her to Pam Baldwin's apartment. He'd thought, as uneasy as she'd seemed, that she might perform a cursory look, but she'd been thorough and had determined that nothing else had been disturbed.

With the sun setting and the temperatures falling, the roads had frozen over, and Jake kept his attention on driving and watching to see if anyone followed them. As he parked in the lot of the modest apartment complex in a neighborhood very close to Rachael's child development center, he could confidently say that they hadn't been followed. Still, the kidnapper could know Ms. Baldwin's address, so Jake wouldn't let down his guard.

"Thank you for bringing me over here," Rachael said as she unbuckled her seat belt. "The doctor said the drug wouldn't be completely out of my system for twenty-four hours, and I shouldn't drive until then."

"Good advice."

"He also told me not to sign any legal documents, so if you're planning to get me to sign a confession, that'll have to wait until tomorrow." She smiled sweetly.

Her change in attitude surprised him, but he didn't

question it and returned her smile. "Bummer. I was going to haul you in right after this visit."

Still grinning, she opened the door, and a rush of cold air settled into the cab. Rachael shivered and tightened her coat before stepping out. He met her on the sidewalk and they hurried to Apartment C located on the ground level of the two-story building.

Jake noted the flaking paint and cracked sidewalks. He hadn't expected Ms. Baldwin's place to be five-star, not when she worked a minimum-wage job and needed assistance for her child care.

He knocked and stepped back to wait.

"Yeah?" a cautious female voice said from the other side of the door.

"It's me, Pam." Rachael stepped in front of Jake so Ms. Baldwin would see her through the peephole.

"Rachael," Ms. Baldwin squealed, and the dead bolt clicked open. As tall as Jake, the woman had long black hair and big blue eyes. She ran her gaze over Rachael from head to toe. "You're okay. Really okay."

"Yes," Rachael said.

Ms. Baldwin grabbed Rachael in a hug, shaking her like a rag doll. Jake saw Rachael wince, likely from bruises sustained in her attack, but she didn't cry out and Ms. Baldwin continued to hold her tight.

"I'm sorry to bother you," Rachael said, a bit more formally than he expected. "But I really needed to see Kelly. Just to see that's she fine, too."

Ms. Baldwin let Rachael go and stepped back. "She's sleeping. Come on in."

"This is Deputy Jake Marsh," Rachael said offhandedly as she passed the other woman. "He's one of the deputies who scared off the kidnapper."

"Then I'm pleased to meet you." Ms. Baldwin grabbed

his hand and gave it a very manly shake. "You're most welcome in my house anytime."

"Nice to meet you, too, Ms. Baldwin."

She waved a hand. "None of this Ms. stuff. It's Pam, okay?"

"Okay," he said.

She ushered him inside. Worn carpet in a hideous green color covered the floors, but the place looked clean and smelled good. Pam was doing the best she could with what she had. The furnishings were of excellent quality, which he found odd on her salary, but he suspected the items had been given to her.

"Can I peek in on Kelly?" Rachael asked immediately. "I won't pick her up, but I have to see her."

"Sure," Pam replied.

Rachael opened a door on the right and tiptoed inside, but left the door open a crack.

"Sit," Pam commanded as she dropped into a high-quality leather recliner.

Jake perched on the arm of a matching sofa in case Rachael needed him.

"So you saved the day, huh?" Pam asked.

Jake shared as much of the rescue story as he could. "My team is the best."

"Then thank them for me, and if there's anything I can do to repay you, just name it."

"Tell me about Rachael."

"Rachael? Sure, yeah. She's, like, this amazing person who's helped me so much. After I got clean, I lived in a state-supported home. Then I had Kelly, and I really wanted a place of our own, you know? Meant I had to get a job so I could afford a place, but to work, I needed child care."

She paused and seemed lost in her thoughts for a moment. "Most directors turned their noses up at me. No job meant no tuition. Rachael was the opposite. She said she'd hold a slot for Kelly, and she'd be glad to take her while I looked for work and wouldn't charge me a thing. I mean, can you imagine that? Free child care so we could get a leg up? Crazy, right?"

"Crazy good," Jake replied.

Pam nodded vigorously. "That was just the beginning. She vouched for me to get this place. Gave me all the great furniture and most of the dishes and things I needed to get set up here." Pam shook her head. "She said she was downsizing from her old life and had this stuff in storage. Guess her husband, before he died, was some kind of executive and made lots of money, and they once had a humongous house." A broad smile claimed Pam's mouth. "You don't run into people like her very often."

"No, you don't." Jake stared at the doorway and wished she'd return.

"She's cared for Kelly ever since then, and when I'm short on money, she helps by letting me pay my tuition late if needed." Pam frowned. "I just don't know what I'm going to do if she can't open the center again."

Rachael stepped back into the room and softly closed the door. "I wanted to talk to you about that."

"Hey, no worries," Pam said. "You've got a lot on your plate. I'll figure it out."

"I already have an idea." Rachael sat on the sofa next to Pam. "My mother's friend just retired. I can give Francie a call, and I'm sure she'll be glad to watch Kelly until I can reopen the center."

Jake hid his surprise at her statement. From the way the call to her licensing rep went, it sounded like she might never reopen. Maybe she really thought they'd lift the suspension, or she was simply putting on a good front for Pam so she didn't worry. That seemed just like the kind of thing the Rachael he was getting to know would do.

"Are you sure?" Pam asked. "You've already done so much for me, and I hate to take advantage of one of your mother's friends."

"You're not taking advantage, and I'll keep offering help until you no longer need it."

Pam gave Rachael a one-armed hug. "You are such a blessing. God really smiled on me the day He put you in my life."

Jake expected Rachael to smile or at least look pleased at the compliment, but she looked away instead and dug out her phone that they'd stopped to pick up on the way to Pam's apartment.

"Let me call Francie now." Rachael extracted herself from the hug and got up to go into the miniscule kitchen with old avocado-colored appliances.

"See?" Pam said. "I told you she's the best."

"Yes, she is," Jake agreed as he continued to study her.

Jake couldn't figure Rachael out. She was loving and caring—that much was obvious—but when someone returned the same sentiments, she backed away and acted like she didn't deserve it.

He doubted it had to do with the investigation, but that didn't matter. She so intrigued him that while he made sure she stayed safe, he would do his very best to discover what made her tick.

Rachael received an affirmative response from Francie just as she'd expected. She returned to the sofa. Jake was deep in conversation with Pam, so Rachael used the time to jot down Francie's contact information.

"Do you mind if I ask you a few questions about Kelly?" Jake asked.

Pam cast him a wary look. Rachael knew the feeling from her earlier interview with the detective.

"Go ahead," Pam said.

"Could you tell me about Kelly's father?"

"I'm not proud of this, but I don't know who he is." She took a deep breath and lifted her chin. Pam was a proud woman and the topic had to be difficult for her.

"I was once a real mess," she added. "But I've given my life to God now, and He forgives me. That means I can hold my head up high."

"Hey." Jake held up his hand. "No judgment here. Everyone makes mistakes, and if not for the grace of God, we would all crumble under our guilt." He spoke with confidence, but the conviction didn't travel to his eyes, as if he didn't really believe his own words.

"I was in a bad place then," Pam continued. "I was so strung out, but there were a coupla guys I hung with on a regular basis." She huffed a sour laugh. "As much as my little drug family could hang out, that is. I gave their names to your detective, but we never had a home base, so it may be hard to track them."

"Did any of them have a record?"

"Sure, we all did."

"For what?"

"Me...possession. The guys had burglary added to their rap sheets."

"Anything violent?"

"Sid had some bad stuff before I knew him. I'm not sure of the details, but he went away for longer than me and Hal."

By *away*, Rachael knew Pam meant to prison, and Jake would know that, too.

"Do you think if either one of them realized Kelly could be his child, he'd want to have her in his life?" Jake asked.

"Not if they haven't gotten clean." She lifted her face in thought. "If they're still using and they know I have a baby, they'd try to figure out how we could use her to help score money for drugs."

"As in try to kidnap and sell her?" Rachael tried to hide the shock in her voice, but failed.

"Maybe... I don't know." Pam gnawed on her lower lip. "I was thinking more along the lines of scamming government programs to get extra money. When I was on the street, I saw people illegally using food stamps and welfare checks." She twisted her fingers together. "But I guess we can't rule out the kidnapping thing, either. When someone is jonesing for their next fix, they'd do just about anything to get it. So, yeah, maybe they would."

"Trust me, I've seen the extremes addicts have employed to score drugs," Jake said. "But kidnapping a child takes planning, and a person continually high on drugs usually doesn't have the wherewithal to plan such a thing."

"That's so true," Pam replied, relief flowing through her tone.

"Any other ideas about who might have tried to take Kelly?"

Pam shook her head. "You ever think this had nothing to do with Kelly at all? That maybe she was just in the wrong place at the wrong time?"

"We are considering that possibility," Jake answered. "Still, in case this is specifically related to Kelly, I need you to be extra careful."

"Yeah, I thought about that." She chewed on her lip

again. "I'm kinda worried about the morning when I go to work. If I go to work." She looked at Rachael.

"You're all set with Francie."

"Thank you." Pam squeezed Rachael's hand. "Does she live nearby?"

"Unfortunately, no." Rachael handed the address to Pam.

She looked at it, then shrugged. "I'll just get an earlier start and be careful, like you said." She peered at Jake. "There aren't many people around at that time of day, and it's dark. I'll probably freak out walking to the bus stop, but it'll be okay."

"You don't have a car?" he asked.

She shook her head.

"Then I'll pick you up," he offered. "We can drop off Kelly first, and then I'll drive you to work."

"You'd do that for me?" Pam asked.

"Sure, why not? I'm not usually on duty at that time of day unless we have a callout. If that happens, I'll arrange for someone else to pick you up."

"If it was just me, I wouldn't ask, but Kelly..." Pam's eyes lit with love for the baby.

Rachael's heart warmed at seeing how Pam had overcome so much due to love for her child. Jake's offer warmed her heart, as well. Just like that, he'd agreed to give a stranger a ride to work, or at least arrange for a ride. He continued to prove he was a great guy, albeit one who seemed to carry a burden that left him reserved at times.

Kelly's cries sounded from her room. Rachael didn't like to hear the little sweetheart cry, but she did like that she was awake, giving Rachael a chance at snuggles before they left.

Pam started to get up, but Rachael stopped her. "Can I do it? I'd like to spend a little time with her before we go."

"Sure." Pam winked. "And you can come back in the middle of the night, too, if you want."

Laughing, Rachael warmed the bottle in the kitchen, then took it to Kelly's room. She felt Jake's gaze track her every movement, and she wondered what he was thinking. He hadn't acted like he really believed she was involved in the kidnapping attempt. In fact, neither had Detective Hunter when she'd taken Rachael's statement at the house. A pleasant surprise, and Rachael had to admit she was beginning to like the detective.

Rachael slid her hands under Kelly's warm little body. She lifted the precious bundle to her shoulder, and Kelly's cries stilled. She was such an easy baby, and Rachael loved caring for her.

She snuggled the sweet girl close and kissed her downy head. "I'm so glad you're all right, little one. I was terrified for you. But now you have Jake on your side, too. He'll keep you safe."

Rachael changed Kelly's diaper, then put her back in the crib so she could quickly wash her hands in the next-door bathroom before settling into the recliner with Kelly. Her baby-soft scent drifted up, and love overflowed Rachael's heart. She hadn't lied when she'd told Detective Hunter that Kelly wasn't more special than the other children she cared for. But as the youngest, Kelly was the most vulnerable and needed more attention. Rachael was happy to lavish that attention on her.

Kelly suckled her bottle and curled her tiny fingers around Rachael's index finger. As she stared into the baby's big blue eyes, she could hear the low rumble of Jake's voice in the other room. He'd been such a godsend today, and she appreciated everything he'd done for her.

What she didn't appreciate was that since meeting him thoughts about Eli and the loss of the baby she and Eli had planned to name Hannah continued to plague her.

What a horrible night that had been. Eli died on Christmas Eve, and all the light went out in her world. She'd abandoned all hope, falling into despair. She couldn't eat. Couldn't sleep. Couldn't focus. Eli had been her whole life. Cared for her and provided for the family. Though she had a business degree, he'd made enough money that she hadn't really needed a job, and once she discovered her pregnancy, she quit work to get ready for the baby.

One month almost to the day after he died, she miscarried their child. The doctor said she wasn't to blame, but because she was in such poor physical shape from losing Eli, she'd felt responsible. She still felt responsible and blamed herself.

If only Eli hadn't been such a generous man and offered to go to the store for her ice-cream craving, he'd be alive. And if she'd taken better care of herself, Hannah would be alive. Rachael would be alive inside, too.

If only, if only, if only. She'd traveled that path too many times, and it would do no good to take it again.

Kelly suddenly startled, drawing Rachael's attention. The pain from her miscarriage came flooding back, the loss still vivid in her heart. No matter how many children and families she helped, the visceral ache would live with her for the rest of her life. Which was why this interest in Jake would go nowhere. She might find him appealing and interesting, but she wouldn't get involved with him or any man. Even if she deserved a family, which she didn't, she wouldn't risk such heartbreak again.

She hummed a song and kept her gaze on Kelly while she finished her bottle. Then she burped and rocked her until she heard the child's even breathing. Rachael didn't want to get up and leave the solitude of the room, didn't want to leave Kelly, but it was unfair for Jake to have to wait around much longer.

She kissed Kelly's silky hair, then placed her in her crib. "Sleep tight, little one."

She crept out of the room and found Jake stowing his phone in his pocket.

"We should get going," she said, then faced Pam. "Let me know if you have any questions, or if there are any problems with locating Francie's apartment."

Pam got up and escorted them to the door. Rachael made sure to stay behind Jake so Pam couldn't hug her again. She loved getting hugs from her families, but her ribs were so sore that she couldn't handle another one of Pam's bear hugs.

They said goodbye and hurried through the nippy cold to Jake's truck. Once they were settled and he had the heat cranked up, he turned to her. "Would you like to come back to our firehouse for dinner?"

"Firehouse?"

"Oh, right, you don't know," he said. "Our team. We all live together in a historic firehouse that was remodeled especially for us. We each have our own condo on the second floor, and the first floor has a kitchen, game room and family room that we can share when we want."

"Sounds nice."

"It is, and it's worth coming over just to see the place. A woman named Winnie Kerr donated it to the county with the sole purpose of housing our team. She did a first-rate renovation while still keeping many of the firehouse elements in place."

"That's quite generous."

"It's in appreciation for our medic, Darcie Stevens, saving Winnie's life."

"So, do you dine with the team or alone?"

"Oh, you mean tonight? Will we be alone?"

She nodded.

"No, it's a team thing." He frowned as he seemed to realize she didn't want to be alone with him.

She didn't really want to have dinner with strangers, either, but she couldn't bear going back to her home that had been violated by not only the kidnapper but also the forensic staff, who'd left fingerprint powder everywhere.

"Dinner sounds nice," she said.

At his wide smile her heart rate kicked up, and she hoped she hadn't just made a very big mistake.

SIX

Jake shifted into gear and ignored the way caution took over Rachael's expression. He wanted to ask about the change, but he thought it best not to delve into anything personal. Especially not after the way she'd resembled a trapped animal when she'd thought dinner might be just the two of them. She'd made it crystal clear that she didn't want to be alone with him. Maybe she just wasn't into dating yet, and she thought he was coming on to her. He needed to rectify that.

"Tell me more about your team," she said, falling right in line with his intent to keep things on a professional level.

"I think I mentioned that there are six of us on the team. We're pretty unique, as very few agencies have a first response team with our makeup. I told you Detective Hunter is a negotiator, but we have a second one, too, because most of our callouts involve negotiations of some sort. Archer Reed is the other negotiator, and then we have a sniper, a bomb tech and a paramedic."

"Wow," she said. "Were all of these people at the center today?"

He shook his head. "We were on the way to a tactical training session, so only Cash and Brady were with me.

I would have loved to have the others, though, because we work best as a full team."

"How did you get involved in such a group?" she asked. "No, wait, start with how you became a deputy."

He glanced at her, and it didn't appear as if she was making small talk, but she seemed genuinely interested in his answer.

"I guess it started when I was thirteen," he said. "My dad worked at the US embassy in Nairobi. He, my mom and my brother and sister were all killed when it was bombed."

"Oh, Jake, I'm sorry. That must have been so hard."

Her sincerity raised feelings he'd thought he'd dealt with long ago. He swallowed them down and continued by focusing on the positive. "It was tough, but it gave me direction for my life. I should have been at the embassy that day, but I snuck out to hang with some friends my parents didn't like."

"And you feel guilty for surviving," she said, as if she knew something about survivor's guilt.

"I can't help but think if I'd been there, I might have saved them somehow."

"But you were only a kid."

"Still, I wonder, you know?"

"Yes, I definitely know."

"Because of your husband?"

She nodded but looked away. Jake suspected there was something more to her story that she didn't want to share.

"Anyway," Jake continued, "at my parents' funeral, I promised them that I would help people faced with a sudden crisis. Becoming a law enforcement officer seemed like a good way to do that."

"And I suppose your team does that more than most officers."

"Exactly. When the opportunity came up to form and lead the team, I knew God custom-made it for me."

"And has the job been what you thought it would be?"

He'd never really thought about it so he considered her question for a moment. "I feel good about what we do. Sometimes we've been able to extend our help beyond the emergency. For example, our team medic, Darcie Stevens, saved a young girl's life in a callout. Now Darcie and her fiancé, Noah, are in the process of adopting Isabel."

"That's wonderful," Rachael said.

"Yeah, it's great, but I don't want to mislead you. The job can also be more heartbreaking than I imagined it would be."

She nodded, then looked out the window. He opted to remain quiet and wait for any additional questions she might have, but she didn't speak.

He'd liked talking with her. Even sharing about his family, as she seemed to understand. But it was probably a good thing that she'd clammed up. They'd entered the personal realm when they needed to stay focused on the attempt to kidnap Kelly.

He turned his attention back to driving and was glad that she remained silent for the rest of their drive.

"We're here," he announced as he approached the old firehouse that still made him smile when he drove up.

The building sat back from the road, with pine trees soaring to the sky on either side of a wide driveway. Winnie made sure the redbrick exterior and two original fire doors were preserved. The team, under Skyler's direction, had strung garland around the entrance. Icicle lights dangled from the eaves, and multicolored lights sparkled from the large pines.

"Wow," Rachael said, a smile in her voice. "This is so picturesque."

"It's a nice thing to come home to after a hard day." He pulled into the wide driveway and shifted into Park.

"Nice?" She shot him a quick look. "It's like a winter wonderland." She clapped her hands together in glee.

He was thrilled that the sight of his home brought her joy after her difficult day.

"With the crazy, snowy winter we've been having, I can just see it falling softly from the sky and glittering in all of these lights." She swiveled to look at him. "Oh, and a sleigh. Wouldn't it be amazing to arrive here in a sleigh?"

He stared at her eyes the color of green sea glass and loved how full of life she appeared.

She chuckled. "I guess I let my imagination run wild some times."

"It's probably part of your job, right? Working with children all day."

She nodded. "And my parents. They loved Christmas and always made it special for me."

"Loved?"

Her smile fell, making him regret asking the question.

"They've both passed away. They were in their forties when they had me, so I lost them way too early, but I have such fond memories of them. My dad especially loved to make a big deal of holidays, and we often rented a cabin in the mountains for Christmas. It was so spectacular. I can still hear the horse hooves pawing the ground and the jingle of the bells on the reins when we went for rides on winding mountain roads."

"Sounds nice." He opened the door. "I've never been real big on Christmas."

They both got out, and Jake led the way up the sidewalk. He opened a solid oak door holding a pine wreath that freshened the air and stepped back. Rachael entered the foyer. She ran her fingers over the garland coiling up a black metal banister that led to a second-floor balcony. Red bows were scattered among white lights and large silver balls dangled below. Each step held a poinsettia, and a two-story tree loaded with decorations filled the corner.

"Wow. Just wow." Rachael turned in circles, her gaze going over every inch of the place. "You said you've never been big on Christmas, but this? Do you decorate like this every year?"

"Me, no," he replied. "It's all Skyler's doing. She hosts an annual Christmas party for homeless children, and every year she outdoes the prior year's decorations."

"As in Detective Hunter?" Rachael muttered. "I would never have imagined."

"I told you she was quite a woman," Jake said.

Rachael nodded, but didn't look convinced.

She had to be fully aware of Skyler's tough investigator side after Skyler'd had to ask very difficult questions. He hoped coming here would help Rachael see Skyler's caring and compassionate side, too, and for some reason he couldn't put a finger on, he wanted Rachael to like his friends as much as he did.

Jake moved ahead, but Rachael couldn't quit taking in the amazing building. He continued to be patient with her and eventually he led her into a massive open area abutting the large doors where she assumed the trucks had once parked. She checked out the polished concrete floors, then swung her gaze over even more decorations. Voices echoed against the first floor's high ceilings, carrying ductwork and pipes across the space.

Suddenly apprehensive about the decision to come here, she grabbed Jake's arm.

"Wait," she said. "I'm not sure this is a good idea."

"Why not?"

"After the day I've had, socializing might be a challenge. Especially with people involved in this investigation."

"Relax." He smiled and squeezed her hand. "We're just regular people outside of work. Like a family. You'll be fine."

He pressed his hand at the small of her back and urged her into the room with big sofas, recliners and leather club chairs. The voices came from the adjoining kitchen where men, women and a young girl gathered around an island. Rachael quickly scanned the room for Detective Hunter and was pleased to see she wasn't in attendance.

Jake went around to the far side of the island, putting his hand on shoulders and introducing the group. Team members Cash Dixon, Archer Reed and Darcie Stevens were present, along with Cash's wife, Krista, and Archer's fiancée, Emily. Isabel sat on a stool next to her biological grandmother, Pilar.

"I've already told Rachael about all of you," Jake said.

They all groaned. A temptation to say something funny to break the ice hit Rachael, but she didn't know these people, so she held her tongue.

Jake took over the conversation, describing the kidnapping and sharing the break-in.

Darcie dropped her cookie cutter and came around the island to squeeze Rachael's arm. "You poor thing. Would you like to join us in cookie decorating, or would you rather just sit down and eat a bunch of them?"

Tall and slender with wavy hair pulled back into a ponytail, Darcie's brown eyes filled with compassion. Despite her day, Rachael instantly felt better under Darcie's attention.

Isabel jumped down from her stool and took Rachael's hand. "You look like you need Christmas. You can have my stool."

Rachael smiled at the child as she led Rachael to the stool. She sat, and Pilar pushed to her feet. A large puppy that looked nearly full grown came loping into the room and tried to stop near Isabel, but slid past her and hit the wall instead.

"That's Woof," Isabel said, her tone serious. "He's my dog. He doesn't stop so good."

Pilar shook her head, but with a fond smile on her face, she turned to Rachael. "It was nice to meet you. I am praying for a resolution to your problems." She patted Rachael's shoulder before looking at her granddaughter. "Come, Isabel. We have some wrapping to do."

Isabel giggled and winked at Darcie. "Do not come upstairs. And when Noah comes home from work, do not let him come up, either."

Darcie smiled down on the child and took a few exaggerated steps like she might follow. Isabel raced away, giggles trailing behind.

Rachael instantly liked Darcie. Rachael suspected it was because Darcie was a former nurse turned medic, and the same warm, caring personality she used on the job shone through in her personal life.

Jake slid onto the stool vacated by Pilar. His body consumed the space, and when his knee touched Rachael's, she scooted away to keep from thinking of how his touch affected her heart.

He grabbed a snowman-shaped cookie, chomped off a bite and moaned. "Perfect as usual, Darcie."

She laughed. "You sound surprised that I'm good for more than poking people with needles."

"How could he be surprised?" Archer nodded at the

stove where a large pot sat on the front burner. "You're the only one in the group who actually knows how to cook."

"Hey," Cash said. "I take offense at that. I can order a mean pizza."

"Which we'll be eating tomorrow night again," his wife, Krista, added.

"You could take over my cooking duties, honey." He smiled at her, and she beamed back at him.

The pure look of love in their eyes brought back Rachael's memories of Eli. She didn't think she could experience a love like that again, but she still liked to witness it in other people, and Cash and Krista obviously shared a forever kind of love.

Darcie slid a pan of plain star-shaped cookies across the island. "We decorate freestyle, so help yourself to anything on the island."

Jake picked up a cookie and a decorating bag filled with blue icing. Rachael chose yellow frosting, and as she slathered it on the cookie, she kept peeking at Jake's decoration. He covered his cookie in blue then quickly wrote FRS in the middle in yellow and set it aside.

"Really, Jake?" Darcie asked. "Your focus may be on work all the time, but it's Christmas. Where's your spirit?"

He looked up and frowned at Darcie. "Fine. Give me something other than a star, and I'll do my best."

She handed him a tree, but his frown didn't leave his face until he piped the icing in dots to mimic ornaments. Then his tongue peeked out the side of his mouth, and he fixed his rapt attention on the tree. Every so often he'd sit back to eye it, then add a bit more. Finally he pressed silver balls into the dots and pushed back from the counter.

"There," he said, a broad smile on his face. "I challenge anyone to do better."

"A challenge? I can get all over a challenge," Cash said. "Give me a tree, Darcie."

She passed the plate to him and looked at Archer.

He held up his hands. "Hey. I don't need to prove my cookie-decorating abilities."

"Since when does anyone on the team shy away from a challenge?" Jake's smile morphed into a visual taunt.

"Since it involves icing and precision," Archer replied.

"Too bad Brady's not here," Krista said. "With his sharpshooting and whittling skills, he'd give you precision."

Rachael had to admit she was having fun with the team, though she wished she could share their enthusiasm for Christmas. She'd even settle for a spark, a mere flicker of Christmas sprit. Sure, she could still appreciate the beauty of seasonal decorations like Skyler's, as it reminded her of great Christmases with her parents, but since she lost the baby and Eli, the thought of a traditional Christmas celebration still left her feeling cold inside.

The sound of the front door opening caught Darcie's attention. "Maybe that's him now."

They all swiveled to look, but when Detective Hunter and a tall, striking man wearing a black suit entered the room, Rachael's thoughts turned back to the attempted kidnapping, and her good mood evaporated.

The detective approached the counter, her eyes narrowed, her expression grim. Jake's smile melted away, and he stood, putting his hands on his hips.

Detective Hunter met Rachael's gaze. "Our team has finished processing your center."

"Does that mean I can go inside?"

"Yes. I'm officially releasing the place to you."

Rachael turned to Jake. "Would you mind driving me over there after dinner so I can prepare for my licensing visit?"

He shoved his hands in his pockets. "It's safer to wait until morning."

"You think the kidnapper might come back?" she asked, but the rigid set of Jake's jaw held his answer.

Gone was the lighter, easygoing man who had just issued a cookie-decorating challenge, and back was the fierce defender.

She hated to see the change in him, but she had to admit she was thankful he'd decided to defend her from this crazy kidnapper who seemed like he'd keep coming back until he got what he was after.

Jake drove Rachael home and parked near the patrol car in front of her house. He thought of the mess inside and didn't want her to face it alone, so he turned to her. "If you'll give me your keys, I'll do a walk-through of the house while you wait here with the deputy."

She didn't take any time to think about it, but dug the keys from her purse and held them out.

He took the ring making sure not to touch her. He'd accidentally bumped her leg at the house and the shock of his intense response still lingered. "If you'll also tell me where you keep your cleaning supplies, I can clean off that mirror so you don't have to look at it again."

"That would be so kind of you. You'll find them under the kitchen sink."

"I'll be right back." He opened the door.

"Jake," she said.

He turned. "Yeah?"

"Be careful."

The simple warning evaporated his desire to keep

things professional between them. Sure, taking extra care was always an unspoken thought among the team, but it had been a long time since a woman outside the team had been concerned for his safety.

He knew he shouldn't, but he squeezed her hand. Her eyes widened, and her lips formed a small O of surprise. He figured she was responding to the unexpected warmth traveling between them.

Once again, he hadn't thought a simple touch would affect him this way. She, however seemed immune, as apprehension darkened her eyes. He had to admit her response stung, but he wouldn't even contemplate discussing their differing reactions.

He climbed out of the truck and Deputy Hill met him at the bumper.

Thankful for the distraction to move his focus back to Rachael's safety, Jake greeted the deputy. "Has everything been quiet here?"

"Nothing to report." Hill widened his stance. "Are you any closer to getting this guy?"

Jake shook his head. "So keep your head on a swivel and check out everything, even the littlest thing, okay?"

"Roger that."

"Ms. Long is going to sit in my truck while I do a walk-through of the house, so stay close to her."

Hill nodded. Thankfully, he wasn't treating this assignment as a chance to zone out, but was giving his all. Jake strode up to the porch, his gaze searching each shadow and fixing on every movement of the wind until he'd entered the house. Though it was likely overkill, he drew his weapon and flipped on the lights.

He traveled through the rooms, searching then double-checking. Rachael's safety was too important to miss any clue of another intrusion. Once certain no one lurked inside, he checked the window locks, then searched the backyard and garage. Confident in her home's security, he cleaned off the mirror then returned to his truck and escorted Rachael to the door.

She stood in the open doorway, looking up at him, her gaze questioning. Maybe she didn't want to be alone after her difficult day. He didn't blame her, but it couldn't be helped.

"Are you sure you don't want to call a friend to stay with you?"

"And put them in danger? No."

He totally understood her reasoning. He'd do the same thing in her place. "I'm sorry I have to go. With the time I'll need to devote to you and Pam in the morning, I have to get some work done tonight."

"It's okay. You've done so much already. I wouldn't dream of asking you to do more."

"It's just…" He ran a hand through his hair. "I want to stay…but others. They're depending on me, too."

"I understand."

He nodded and bid her good-night, but he suspected she didn't fully grasp his reason for leaving. It couldn't be helped, though. Deputy Hill would keep her safe, and Jake had to be where people needed him the most. He'd committed his life to that, and so far it had served him and others well.

So why, he thought as he stepped toward his truck, was he questioning his purpose and direction after all these years?

SEVEN

Morning couldn't have come any faster for Rachael, and she was glad to be in Jake's truck headed for the center so she could get to work and keep her mind busy. She'd startled at the littlest sound and spent a sleepless night. When Jake arrived on her doorstep looking tired but still projecting his fierce protector vibe, it was all she could do not to throw her arms around his neck and hold on to him.

"You're awful quiet this morning," he said. "Is something wrong?"

She shook her head, but something was very wrong. She kept responding to him in ways she'd never expected to feel again, and she had to face facts. They had a connection, and it wasn't one-sided.

Going forward, every time they were together, she had to do a better job of keeping their focus on the investigation. That should solve the problem.

Starting right now.

"Pam called to say she dropped Kelly at Francie's place and got to work just fine thanks to your deputy," Rachael said. "Thank you for arranging it, and tell him thanks for me, too."

"Will do."

"Did you get all of your work done last night?" she asked.

"Does anyone ever finish all their work?"

"I do," she said. "I mean, within reason. If I didn't have any down time, I'd fall apart."

"What do you like to do in your down time?"

"Do?" She considered his question. "I babysit a lot."

He cast a surprised look at her. "And that's not work?"

"I don't charge for it, so I don't consider it work." She thought about the hours spent with the children and smiled. "I love it, actually. Children. There's nothing better."

"Sounds like you want to have your own someday."

An innocent comment, but it brought back the day she'd lost Hannah and Rachael couldn't respond. He kept glancing at her, but she avoided his gaze and sought a safe topic.

"The center is just ahead," she managed to get out through a dry mouth.

She stared out the window to end the conversation, and hoped he'd think her sudden quietness had to do with the attempted kidnapping.

They drove down the familiar tree-lined street located in an older, established neighborhood. When she spotted the center—her second sanctuary that had been invaded by the man who tried to kill her—a wave of anxiety actually took over her thoughts of Hannah.

Jake drove closer, and Rachael's mouth fell open. Several Portland TV station vans with call letters brightly painted on the sides and satellite dishes on their roofs were parked on the street. When Jake pulled into the parking lot, reporters she recognized from the news flooded from the vans, their microphones held at the ready.

She pivoted to look at Jake. "I didn't expect this."

"Don't pay any attention to them." Jake eased his truck past the group and parked by the door. "We'll walk straight through and not say a word." He shifted into Park. "Stay here until I come around for you."

She nodded, but when a particularly aggressive reporter from a local news broadcast rushed up to Jake, it left her wondering if getting through the reporters would be as easy as Jake claimed.

He opened the door, stood strong and blocked the reporter's access to her. The moment her feet hit the pavement, he urged her to move quickly ahead of him to the entrance.

"Ms. Long!" the reporter shouted. "Is it true that your license has been suspended for gross negligence?"

The question stopped her. She had been negligent, yes, but he made it sound so ugly. She turned to correct the misconception.

"Let it go," Jake whispered, and took the keys from her hand to unlock the door.

It seemed like an eternity as she waited for the lock to click. When Jake pulled the door open, she rushed inside. The reporter continued tossing out questions until the door closed solidly behind Jake.

She went straight to her office. Catching sight of black forensic powder covering most surfaces, she almost burst into tears.

How could this be happening to her? She was a good person. One who only wanted to help struggling families get a leg up in the world—and now all of this?

Why, Father? Why?

"Sorry about the mess." Jake leaned against the doorjamb.

Rachael dropped onto her desk chair. "The mess is bad, but reporters? I didn't expect them." She shook her head. "I see people on the news all the time and wonder how they ended up there. Never in my wildest dreams did I ever think I'd be one of them."

"I should have thought to warn you. We respond to so many critical incidents that we take it for granted that the press will show up, so I didn't even think about it." He pushed off the door frame. "Why don't we concentrate on getting this space cleaned up so when your licensing rep arrives, she'll get a good first impression?"

"Sounds like a plan." She slipped out of her jacket, then snapped on the lamp on the corner of her desk, illuminating the kid-sized building blocks of the lamp's base. "I'll just grab cleaning products and be right back."

She brushed past Jake, very aware of his presence in her personal space. Her sanctuary had been invaded by not only the kidnapper but also another kind of man. One who seemed to be decent, caring and compassionate. One who put others above himself. Like yesterday, working until the wee hours of the morning.

She pulled open the supply closet door, thoughts of Jake still lingering. He actually reminded her of her father in many ways. He never asked for anything for himself, but was always ready and willing to help others. That's where the similarity ended, though. Her father had been a gentle soul. Slow to act. Indecisive. But Jake? He could change thoughts on a dime, moving into action and taking charge. Unfortunately, she liked that about him, too.

She groaned over her wayward mind, jerked the supplies from the closet and marched back to her office. She had ninety minutes to clean the place up, and she'd do her very best to make the office spotless.

She put the cleaning bottles and paper towels on the desk, then began clearing it. She lifted her appointment book, revealing a photograph she hadn't left on her desk.

The photo showed her and Jake arriving at her house last night.

"This is crazy. Who would have taken our picture?" she asked.

Jake moved closer.

"No. Oh, no." She backed away from the desk.

"What is it?" Jake asked.

She pointed at the picture. "The intruder. He left this. He was here again. In the center."

Jake tried to appear calm, but his heart was hammering hard against his chest. He stepped between Rachael and the doorway, so if the intruder remained in the building he'd have to go through Jake to get to her. He grabbed a tissue to protect any fingerprints and lifted the picture to flip it over.

The backside held a message written in black marker.

Aren't you listening, Rachael? Talk to this cop and he will pay.

Rachael gasped and grabbed Jake's arm. He wanted to comfort her, but first he had to determine if they were in any danger.

"I need to ensure we're alone," he said, his hand already going for his gun.

"Alone! Do you think this guy is still here?"

"No, but we can't be too careful." Jake stepped to the door and turned back. "You'll come with me. Normally I'd do this alone, but with all of these doors and rooms connected, he could circle back here while I'm at the far end of the hallway."

"You're scaring me."

"Not my intent." He forced out a smile. "Grab on to

the back of my shirt so I don't have to wonder if you're right behind me."

"But I—"

"You can do this." He squeezed her arm and turned to wait for her to take hold of his shirttail.

She grabbed a fistful, and he eased down the hallway.

Memories of the prior day, the bullets slamming into his vest, made his step falter for a second. He forced the thought to the back of his mind and moved ahead, clearing one room at a time. Each time he opened a door, he heard Rachael draw in a breath and hold it, then once he announced the room was safe, she blew it out. By the time they'd cleared seven rooms and twice as many bathrooms, she must have felt like she'd run a marathon.

He entered the last room, designed for school-age kids. A window was open, but the space was clear.

"You can let go now," he said.

She dropped his shirt and went to the window. "This is how he got in."

Jake nodded.

"I should have come over last night and set the alarm. Then maybe he would have been caught."

"Or you could have run into him," Jake said.

She pulled in another breath.

"I'm sorry to frighten you, but you have to realize how careful you need to be." After this, there was no way he'd let her stay at her house alone, but he would wait to tell her that until he had a plan in place. "I'll call Skyler to get a team out here and arrange to have this window fixed once they're done."

Rachael stood staring for a long moment before pulling back her shoulders. "My licensing rep can't come here now. I'll call her and cancel."

"We can't leave this room or we risk contaminating

the evidence elsewhere. In fact, we should take off our shoes to minimize contamination of this room."

"My rep's number is posted with emergency numbers by the phone. But if we can walk around this space in our stocking feet, why can't we do the same thing in the hallway?"

"First, the phone is only a few steps away. Second, your socks' fibers can introduce evidence to the scene. Booties are clean and won't cause the same problem so we'll remain put until Skyler arrives."

Normally he wouldn't have been quite this concerned about contamination, but they had few forensic leads other than the single hair they'd recovered from Rachael's clothing, and they needed to take extra care in hopes of locating one.

Rachael slipped out of her shoes as he untied his boots. He dug out his cell phone and arranged for Skyler to come right over, then he let his gaze travel around the room. He spotted video cameras discreetly mounted in two corners. He hoped they were functioning last night and had recorded the intruder. Jake would check on that the moment Skyler arrived and gave them booties.

His thoughts went to the picture lying on Rachael's desk. He'd gotten only a quick look at it, but the angle of the camera said the photographer had lurked across the street from her house. It was bad enough that Deputy Hill hadn't seen the guy last night, but with Jake's many years of training and experience it was inexcusable to miss the guy, too.

He could just imagine the creep hiding behind shrubbery in the vacant lot across the road. Hunkering down, his camera in hand. He most likely had his gun at the ready as Jake said good-night to Rachael, completely oblivious to the danger. Then Jake had hopped into his truck and driven off, leaving the man who'd threatened to kill her watching her from across the street.

Grr! Jake had failed and had to learn from his mistake. Do better. Rachael's life depended on him.

She continued to talk with her licensing rep, rescheduling the appointment for tomorrow, and Jake wanted to pace, but he stayed put. He tapped his finger on the table instead, his leg bouncing, until he heard footsteps whispering outside their door. It sounded like someone wearing shoe coverings, but he wouldn't take any chances. He glanced into the hallway, and when he spotted Skyler, he let out a heavy sigh.

She carried extra booties.

"Did you stop in the office to see the picture?" he asked.

She nodded. "I don't much like that the message says our suspect has added you to his sights."

"I can take care of myself."

"I know you can, but I still don't like the expanded threat." She handed the booties to him. "Let's get Ms. Long settled in the staff lounge, and then we can work this scene."

Jake took the booties to Rachael, who put them on without speaking. He escorted her down the hallway, his gaze drifting to the bulletin boards mounted outside each classroom. Santa Clauses, sleighs and Christmas trees were stapled on red and green background paper. At least that's how he interpreted some of the children's artwork, as it was hard to identity many of the pictures in the under-four-years-old category.

He opened the lounge door and waited for Rachael to get settled. "I hate to make you sit here all alone, but—"

"Don't worry," she said. "I'd rather you help Detective Hunter than keep me company."

He thought he noted an added emphasis on the last bit, but maybe he was imagining things.

"I'll check back with you as soon as I can." He left her behind and joined Skyler in the office, where a computer tech already sat behind the computer.

Skyler stared down on the tech and the guy seemed afraid of her.

Jake had to stifle a laugh over the big guy's fear of itty-bitty Skyler.

She turned and looked Jake square in the eye. "I'm sorry. We don't have any video from last night. It's totally my fault. After the techs pulled the video yesterday they didn't restart the system. I should have followed up."

"Things like that happen," Jake said, but he was disappointed that they'd missed the opportunity to record the suspect in action.

"I'll send a crew over to Rachael's house," Skyler said. "Maybe we'll get be able to locate evidence in the spot where the suspect snapped the picture."

"I don't like the fact that this guy returned to her house again." Jake clamped a hand on his neck. "Even worse, I was right there when he came back. How could I have missed seeing him?"

"You're being too hard on yourself. He must have concealed himself in the bushes, and none of us would have known he was there."

"He could've fired on both of us. Rachael might have been…" He wouldn't put the thought into words.

"But he didn't. Likely because you *were* there, as was Deputy Hill."

"I suppose you're right. It's harder to commit murder when you have officers with guns nearby who can shoot back." Jake tried to let go of the vision of the man loitering across the street, but it lingered in his mind.

"He clearly has no idea that Rachael can't remember what he looks like," Skyler said.

"And as each day passes, he's got to be getting more and more paranoid that we'll release a sketch of him to the public."

Skyler frowned. "Which means we should watch for him to escalate. Maybe try to take that shot you were worried about last night."

"Exactly," Jake said, and he vowed to find a way to keep Rachael out of the intruder's sights.

EIGHT

It was no minor feat, but Jake managed to gather the entire team together in the firehouse family room while their significant others hung out with Rachael in the game room. He stood at the fireplace, all eyes fixed on him. It was rare to call a team meeting during the day, especially when Jake's request wouldn't be offered as a supervisor, but a friend.

He took a breath and launched into his speech. "Let me start by telling you to forget I'm your team leader, and ask you to give your honest opinion."

"Will do," Cash said. "But honestly, you being the boss never stopped me in the past."

"Ditto," Brady added.

"Not me, boss man." Darcie smirked. "I'm always respectful of your leadership."

Jake gave them a testy look. He usually appreciated their jokes and ribbing, but not while Rachael's life was on the line.

"Whoa." Archer slid back. "That scowl means you're not at all pleased with us."

"It's not you." Jake shoved his fingers into his hair. "It's the situation. I want to resolve this quickly so I can make other arrangements if needed."

"Then tell us what this is all about." Skyler smiled, but Jake knew that was bound to disappear with his request.

"Rachael Long received a second warning today." Jake told them about the picture left at the center. "I don't think it's a good idea to have her remain in her house alone, so I'd like her to stay here."

Skyler's eyes narrowed. "That's not a good idea on so many levels."

Jake crossed his arms. "Name them."

She took a breath and blew it out. "Number one. She's a suspect in the kidnapping until I prove otherwise."

"You're not moving too fast at the proving otherwise part, are you?" Jake fired back.

She arched a brow and stared at him for a moment. "Is that a slur on my performance?"

He sighed. "I'm just saying you're busy tracking down other leads, too. Besides, if Rachael was truly your top suspect, then you'd focus on her background check, and you're not."

"True," Skyler admitted, albeit reluctantly.

Cash stood and glanced between them. "So you don't think she's involved?"

"As I told Skyler," Jake replied, "if Rachael was on the wrong side of the law, she wouldn't have a license as a child care provider."

"Ah, Jake," Brady chimed in. "Her license has been suspended."

Jake scowled at Brady. "You know what I mean. Point is, she's not a kidnapper, and she needs help now."

"Which brings up my other main objection." Skyler crossed her arms. "You've taken on Rachael as a crusade, and you're too close to the situation to make an impartial decision."

"I beg to differ," Jake replied. "True, I've taken a personal interest in this case."

Cash snorted. "Very personal."

Jake ignored that. "But I can still form an objective opinion. Rachael's in danger, and she needs more protection than a deputy sitting outside her house can provide."

He widened his stance and ran his gaze over his subordinates. "Let's take a moment to remember the other people who have stayed here under our protection. Krista and her grandfather. Isabel and her grandmother."

He faced Brady. "Your fiancée, Morgan, too. We didn't turn them away when their roles in the investigation were uncertain. Why turn your backs now?"

"He has a good point," Darcie weighed in. "I vote to let Rachael stay here."

Cash nodded. "Krista would scalp me if I didn't agree."

Despite the serious discussion, Jake smiled. Of all the men on their team who Jake never imagined would let a woman take charge in his household, it was Cash, but he loved Krista so intensely that he bowed to her wishes most of the time.

Brady grinned at Cash. "Me, too, and not because Morgan would make me do it."

"I'm good with it," Archer said.

Jake looked at Skyler. "Then I guess it's up to you."

"Fine." She tightened her still-crossed arms. "But promise me you'll keep an eye on her, and if there are any hints that she was involved in Kelly's near abduction, you'll tell me."

"I promise," he replied, as he planned to keep an eye on Rachael.

Both eyes, actually. Not only because he found her beautiful and intriguing, but also because she needed his protection, and another life wouldn't be lost on his watch.

* * *

Rachael was having fun—fun!—while a man continued to threaten her life. She owed her change in attitude to Brady's fiancée, Morgan, and Cash's wife, Krista.
They'd taken out a well-used deck of Uno cards and insisted Rachael join them for a game.

At the end of the third game—Rachael had won all
three—Krista sat back and frowned. "You didn't tell us
you were an Uno shark."

Rachael tried not to smile at the indignant comment.
"I thought it went without saying that since I run a child
care center, I play games with the school-age kids all
the time."

"Ah." Morgan nodded. "That explains it."

"Cash and I plan to have kids," Krista said. "But a
center full of them? No way."

"It's really rewarding," Rachael replied. "Especially
when we get to help mold their lives and support their
parents." Rachael felt tears coming on, so she stopped
talking.

"But it's a lot of responsibility, right?" Krista asked.

Rachael forced herself to lighten up. "Parents appreciate picking their kids up in the same condition they
dropped them off in. You know…with all their fingers
and toes, etc."

The women stared at her, so she winked. They realized she was joking and started laughing. But then
Jake stepped into the room, his expression sober, and
the laughter stilled.

"Uh-oh," Krista said. "I recognize that look. I get it
from Brady all the time before he goes on a callout."

"We haven't been called out," Jake said. "But if you
ladies don't mind—"

"You'd like to talk to Rachael," Morgan finished for him.

"And just when we were having such a good time getting to know her." Krista stood. "Or at least getting to know that we should never play games with her."

Rachael offered a smile of gratitude, and as the women departed, they seemed to take the fun out the door with them.

Jake settled on a chair across from Rachael and fiddled with the deck of cards.

"Just come out and tell me what you need to tell me," she said. "You're making me nervous."

"I don't want you to stay at your house tonight. I don't think it's safe."

"But Deputy Hill—"

"Is doing a good job, but with the suspect proving he's very willing to keep coming back, you need more attention than the deputy can provide from a car."

She'd been thinking the same thing, but she didn't want to impose on Jake any further. "I could stay at a hotel. That way he wouldn't know where I was located."

Jake shook his head. "He could find out, and then you'd be putting others in danger. It's the same as bunking with a friend."

"Then what do you suggest?"

"I'd like you to stay at the firehouse. You can have my condo, and I'll bunk on the couch down here."

"Here? But no… I'd… You'd… That's not a good idea," she said, trying to come up with a reason she couldn't stay since she didn't want to discuss how spending more time with each other wasn't a wise move.

His eyes narrowed, but she couldn't tell what he was thinking. "Why isn't it a good idea?"

"You'd all be in danger, too," she finally managed.

"We're law enforcement officers, Rachael. We know how to handle danger."

"What about Krista, Pilar and Isabel? They live here, too, don't they?"

He nodded. "We've already arranged for them to stay with someone else." He pushed the card deck away and slid closer. "I know you're hesitant. If it's because of the chemistry between us, don't let it play into your decision and leave you exposed to potential attacks."

"It sounds like you think this guy is actually going to try to kill me."

"I don't want to worry you, but I think that's a possibility, and you couldn't be in a safer place than with highly trained deputies."

She knew there was more to it than he was saying, and she wished he'd just come out with his thoughts. She studied him, wanting so desperately to see what was going through his mind now, especially since he'd admitted he felt something, too.

But what did she hope to see? That this was a casual flirtation? Something more? Things she wasn't ready for? Or was he really just worried about an imminent attack?

If he feared an attack, she'd be a fool to insist on staying elsewhere. After all, she was a grown woman, and she could control any potential budding romance between them.

Decision made, she firmed her shoulders. "I'll stay here under one condition."

"Name it."

"You need to promise that we'll keep things strictly professional between us."

He ran a hand over his face. "I'll do my best."

It wasn't hard to see he couldn't promise not to slip.

She couldn't promise that, either, and his best would have to be good enough. "Then that's all I can ask for."

Rachael's phone chimed with a text. She dug it from her pocket. The message was from Pam. "Pam's ready to be picked up from work."

"I need to make sure Brady will be here while I'm gone, or find someone else to transport her."

"We should go so I can talk to Francie about keeping Kelly for a few more days," Rachael said, bringing Jake's sharp gaze her way. "Also, if I'm going to be staying here indefinitely, I need to pick up some things at my house."

"Can't Pam or I talk to Francie? Or maybe you could call her."

Rachael shook her head. "I don't want to tread on my friendship with her. She'll agree to help anyone at any time, even if it's not the right thing for her. I need to look her in the eye to see if she's really good with a longer-term care arrangement."

"Why don't we compromise?" Jake suggested. "I'll ask Darcie or Skyler to pick up your clothes, since that's where the suspect is likely to be hanging out, and you can come with me to Francie's place, as he doesn't likely know anything about her."

"That sounds like a perfect solution to me," she said. "I'll just get my jacket and purse."

She didn't give Jake time to rethink his decision, but gathered her things and hurried into the hallway. He escorted her to an SUV he'd borrowed for this afternoon's transport.

Once on the road, he glanced at her. "How are you doing with this added pressure?"

Fear still lingered from his earlier warnings, and she wished she could let it go and trust God more.

"Rachael?" His tone was more insistent.

"I'll get through this," she replied. "I just have to keep remembering that God has a plan for me, and I'll be fine."

He pulled his gaze from the road, his expression one of surprise. "Sounds like your faith is strong."

"Are you a man of faith?"

He nodded.

"Then you know there are times when you're strong and times when you struggle."

"And now you're fine? Even with all of this going on?"

"*Fine* is a relative term. Compared to when I lost Eli, I am fine. When he died, it took me a long time to come to grips with his loss. But after a lot of dialogue with God, I finally figured out He wanted me to get on with my life and help low-income families. Now that's what gets me out of bed in the morning. They're always in need of help, so I can't let setbacks make me waver. I must think of them first."

She peered at him. "I'm like you in that respect, right? One focus. One direction. No distractions. Just work."

He nodded, clamped both hands on the wheel and put his attention on the road. She took it as a signal that he was done talking—and perhaps it also meant he was questioning his single-minded focus.

They picked up Pam, who chattered nonstop on the drive. Rachael responded when necessary, but she mostly stared out the window and watched the sun sinking toward the horizon. By the time Jake turned into the parking lot of Francie's apartment complex, long shadows shrouded the area, making Rachael shiver.

Jake suddenly craned his neck toward the building. Rachael searched ahead and caught sight of two patrol cars in the lot.

"What's going on?" she asked.

"Do you think they're here because of Kelly?" Pam's voice rose toward panic levels.

Jake slammed on the brakes and shifted into Park. "You two wait here and I'll find out. Keep the engine running, and if anyone other than a police officer approaches the car, you take off."

Jake held out his credentials as he met one of the cops at Francie's apartment door. "What's going on?"

The officer hooked his thumbs in his duty belt. "Attempted break-in."

Jake's heart rate kicked up. "Are Francie and the baby okay?"

"Yeah, the guy never got inside. A neighbor saw him trying to jimmy the lock and scared him away."

Was this attempted break-in related to Kelly, or was it a coincidence?

Jake strongly suspected the former.

"Do you have a lot of crime in this complex?" he asked.

The officer shook his head. "Not in this part of town."

So it was likely related to Kelly. "What did the suspect look like?"

The officer described a man identical to the intruder at the center. "He took off in a white or tan Honda Accord, but the neighbor couldn't make out the plate. We have an alert out on the vehicle, but you know how common Accords are, so we aren't holding out hope."

Jake explained the reason for his visit. "I'll be taking Francie and the baby with me."

"My partner's finishing up with her statement now, so she should be good to go in a few minutes."

"Let me tell the mother that her child is fine, and then I'll be back for them." Jake jogged to the car and signaled for Rachael to lower the window.

He explained the situation and tried to play down his unease. "I'll go back for Francie and Kelly, then take you all to the firehouse for safety."

Pam blew out a long breath as if she'd been holding it. "At least Kelly is okay. If anything had happened to her I'd…"

Rachael's eyes narrowed. "Do you think the suspect came for me?"

Jake shook his head. "He'd have to have been following us today to know where you were, and trust me, he didn't follow us."

"Then how did he know Kelly was with Francie?"

"I hate to say this." Jake ground the words out through his frustration. "But I suspect he followed the deputy this morning."

"So he was here to kidnap Kelly."

"Yes," Jake answered, not taking his gaze from her. "It's becoming clear this man's quest is specific to Kelly, and she's in grave danger, too."

NINE

Rachael grabbed a single slice of pizza from the kitchen island and put it on her plate. Sitting down at the table with the entire First Response Squad and their significant others was a first for her, but Jake had called them together to discuss the second kidnapping attempt. She'd never seen the entire team together, and she had to admit, four big, strapping law enforcement guys made her uncomfortable. And, of course, she was still apprehensive of Detective Hunter, not to mention her FBI husband, and Darcie's detective fiancée, Noah.

Francie had opted to stay with her sister in McMinnville, and Pam hung out in Jake's condo, where Kelly slept in her portable crib. Rachael had delivered some pizza to Pam, and now she took her own slice into the dining room, where Skyler was deep in conversation with Jake. They didn't seem to notice she'd entered the room, so she sat in the chair closest to the door. She picked at her pizza but knew she should eat, since with all the craziness they'd all missed dinner, and this late-night snack replaced it.

"I've come up empty on women connected to Ms. Baldwin who've lost a child," Detective Hunter said. "Now that there's been a second attempt on Kelly, we

FREE Merchandise and a Cash Reward† are 'in the Cards' for you!

Dear Reader,

We're giving away FREE MERCHANDISE and a CASH REWARD!

Seriously, we'd like to reward you for reading this novel by giving you **FREE MERCHANDISE** worth over $20 retail plus a CASH REWARD! And no purchase is necessary!

You see the Jack of Hearts sticker above? Paste that sticker in the box on the Free Merchandise Voucher inside. Return the Voucher today... and we'll send you Free Merchandise plus a Cash Reward!

Thanks again for reading one of our novels—and enjoy your Free Merchandise and Cash Reward with our compliments!

Pam Powers

Pam Powers

P.S. Look inside to see what Free Merchandise is **"in the cards"** for you!

W

e'd like to send you two free books like the one you are enjoying now. Your two books have a combined price of over $10 retail, but they are yours to keep absolutely FREE! We'll even send you 2 wonderful surprise gifts and a Cash Reward†. You can't lose!

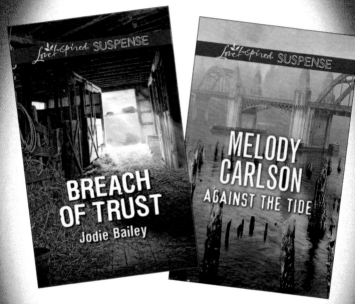

Love Inspired SUSPENSE

BREACH OF TRUST
Jodie Bailey

Love Inspired SUSPENSE

MELODY CARLSON
AGAINST THE TIDE

REMEMBER: Your Free Merchandise, consisting of **2 Free Books** and **2 Free Gifts**, is worth over $20 retail! Plus we'll send you a **Cash Reward** (it's a dollar) which is really the icing on the cake because it's in addition to your FREE Merchandise! No purchase is necessary, so please send for your Free Merchandise today.

Get TWO FREE GIFTS!
We'll also send you 2 wonderful FREE GIFTS (worth about $10 retail), in addition to your 2 Free books and Cash Reward!

Visit us at:
www.ReaderService.com

Books received may not be as shown

YOUR FREE MERCHANDISE INCLUDES...

2 FREE Books **AND** 2 FREE Mystery Gifts
PLUS you'll get a Cash Reward†

FREE MERCHANDISE VOUCHER

2 FREE
BOOKS
and
2 FREE
GIFTS

Please send my Free Merchandise, consisting of
2 Free Books and **2 Free Mystery Gifts** PLUS my
Cash Reward. I understand that I am under no
obligation to buy anything, as explained
on the back of this card.

❑ I prefer the regular-print edition   ❑ I prefer the larger-print edition
153/353 IDL GLJT   107/307 IDL GLJT

Please Print

| |
| FIRST NAME |

| |
| LAST NAME |

| |
| ADDRESS |

| | |
| APT.# | CITY |

| | |
| STATE/PROV. | ZIP/POSTAL CODE |

NO PURCHASE NECESSARY!

SLI-N16-FMC15

know the kidnapper is after her, and this is all tied to Ms. Baldwin somehow."

"I concur," Jake said.

"Maybe it's the grandparents," Skyler said. "When I went back and put the pressure on them, they admitted to knowing about Kelly, and they're angry that Ms. Baldwin has chosen to raise her without telling them about her."

"That's not necessarily a reason to kidnap the child," Archer said. As a negotiator, Rachael thought he must have strong insight into motivations. "But it's the best one we've got so far."

"I really think it's possible," Detective Hunter said. "Not the grandfather himself, mind you, as he doesn't fit the size and build of the kidnapper, but he could have arranged it." The detective took a long drink of water.

Jake slid forward on his chair. "I want to talk to them first thing tomorrow."

The detective set her glass down. "That's not a good idea, Jake. You're too personally involved."

He held up his hand. "My mind's made up, so don't try to talk me out of it."

Rachael saw the frustration on Detective Hunter's face that was pale, her lips drawn. She went to pick up her pizza, then dropped it back on the plate and wrapped her arms around her stomach as if she was ill. Rachael thought about asking how she was feeling, but she didn't want to ask something so personal of a woman who'd made it clear there was nothing personal about their relationship.

Deciding to mind her own business and get through dinner, Rachael took a bite of her pizza and chewed, though she didn't really taste it, her mind on Pam's parents. If they were indeed trying to take Kelly, Pam would be so hurt. She'd also be afraid that they might succeed, and she'd lose Kelly. Rachael wouldn't be surprised if once Pam learned of this, she'd decide to move somewhere the grandparents couldn't find her. Pam couldn't afford to care for Kelly on her own, so what would become of them?

Rachael would have a talk with Pam. If she had any inkling that Pam planned to leave town and Rachael couldn't convince her to stay, she'd make sure Pam left with plenty of money to help her get settled in a new home.

The others started filing into the room, and Cash dropped one of the large pizza boxes in the middle of the table. It was then that Jake seemed to notice Rachael sitting at the table. Darcie, Krista and Morgan entered, talking and giggling about Darcie's upcoming wedding.

At the moment, Rachael would have given almost anything to be that lighthearted again. She lifted the pizza to her mouth, but her lips started tingling, and she dropped the piece on the plate just as her tongue began to tingle, too.

The tingling was a warning sign. She shot a look at the pizza.

"Peanuts," she said, her throat itching. "Could there be peanuts on this pizza?"

"Who ever heard of peanuts on a pizza?" Cash laughed.

"I'm allergic." She felt her throat closing, and her hand came up to scratch at it. "It has… Oh, no. I need my EpiPen."

"Where?" Jake asked.

"Purse…family room," she managed to get out before her airway narrowed more.

Jake bolted to his feet. She heard his footsteps pounding through the kitchen. She tried not to panic as her airway continued to constrict.

Darcie rushed to her side. "Let's get you to the floor."

Rachael knew it was a precaution so that if she passed out from lack of oxygen, she didn't fall and hit her head. That thought made the situation seem more dire. Panic reared up as Darcie and Brady helped her sit on the cold concrete behind the chairs.

Her ears started ringing, and she grew light-headed. A black ring circled the edge of her vision.

Jake charged back into the room.

Rachael's gaze went to his hands. He held the padded case for her pen, but the tight look on his face terrified her.

"The EpiPen," he said, dropping to the floor next to her. "It's missing."

"I have epinephrine in my bag in the equipment room." Darcie jumped up, and Jake nearly shouted out in praise.

"Someone call an ambulance!" she yelled over her shoulder as she ran from the room, moving past the rest of the team members, who had come to their feet and were staring down on Rachael.

"I'll call," Cash offered.

Jake's gut cramped as he took Rachael's hand. Her eyes widened in horror, and she clawed at her throat with the other hand. Her lips had swollen, and her mouth was open, her tongue swelling, too.

His heart creased and panic raced up his back, but he had to hold it together for Rachael.

He squeezed her hand. "Focus on me, honey. Panic will only make it worse."

He felt like a real hypocrite, as his gut churned with acid from his own panic.

She looked into his eyes. Hers were dark with worry, and she gripped his hand tighter.

"It's okay," he said softly. "Darcie will be back in a second, and she'll fix this." He stroked Rachael's hair from her face and forced a smile. "I promise."

She focused on him, but neither that nor his touch replaced her obvious fear of suffocation. She started to thrash around.

Darcie careened into the room, a medical bag slung over her shoulder, an oxygen tank under her arm and a syringe already in her hand.

"Put the mask on her." She shoved the tank at Jake and quickly stuck the needle into Darcie's arm, then pressed the plunger.

Jake strapped the mask over Rachael's mouth. A hint of blue colored her lips, and she continued to gasp for air. He grabbed her hand again and held it tight, his heart thumping so hard he thought Darcie might need to treat him, too.

Darcie rested her hand on Rachael's shoulder. "Give it a few seconds to work."

After several moments, her breathing seemed to ease a bit, and her hand relaxed a fraction in Jake's. She coughed. Breathed deeper. Again and again. Blinked hard.

Darcie strapped on a cuff and took her blood pressure.

"Good," she said. "Are you doing better?"

Rachael nodded, and Jake hissed out a breath, then nearly melted into a puddle on the floor.

Rachael lifted the mask. "Thank you, Darcie. If you didn't have the syringe—"

"No," Jake interrupted and gently settled the mask back into place. "She did, and you're okay."

"You said you're allergic to peanuts?" Darcie clarified. Rachael nodded.

"Peanuts in pizza?" Brady asked. "Cash is right. That's just crazy."

Cash leaned over the table, fumbling with the box, then studying a pizza slice. "I don't see anything."

"You think the shop has an issue?" Darcie asked.

"One way to find out." Cash pulled out his phone and was soon deep in conversation with the pizza store manager.

Everyone else stood looking at Rachael, making Jake even more uncomfortable. Usually so strong in a crisis, his team acted as if they were in shock. Jake got it, though. It was one thing to go to a callout for a stranger, and quite another to have an emergency play out under their own roof with someone they knew.

Rachael stirred and looked like she wanted to get up, but lying there was in her best interest, so Jake remained holding her hand to keep her still.

Cash slammed his phone on the table. "They have no nuts, nor have they ever had a nut in the shop."

"Maybe one of their vendors?"

"No, they make all pizzas from scratch. There's no way the pizza was contaminated at the shop."

"Sabotage?" Jake asked.

"The kidnapper," Skyler said. "But he'd have to know that Rachael has a peanut allergy and then intercept the delivery guy to taint the pizza. Maybe with a few drops of peanut oil."

Cash ground his teeth. "Which means I got the pizza from the kidnapper at the door."

"Darcie, stay with Rachael." Jake jumped to his feet and ran from the room.

He wanted to jerk open the door, but the kidnapper could be outside waiting. He checked out the front window and saw the pizza delivery car still parked in the drive. Cash, Brady and Archer joined him, and he pointed out the car.

"I'll lead," Jake said, without even suggesting that they should check out the car. He knew none of them would stay behind and do nothing. "One of you cover me."

"My mistake," Cash said, his tone frustrated. "I'll take the lead."

He pushed past Jake without regard for his own safety and, holding his weapon at the ready, he proceeded down the driveway.

Jake didn't waste any time, but followed Cash into the chilly night.

"Brady and I'll do a perimeter check," Archer offered, and the pair split up, moving cautiously toward opposite sides of the house.

Jake walked to the car, making sure to sidestep icy spots in the drive and keep alert for any threat. He approached the delivery vehicle, where Cash stared through the back window. Skyler had stepped outside, too, and she joined them.

Jake looked inside the car and spotted a man tied and gagged. Jake could only assume he was the legitimate driver. Jake opened the door and freed the man so they could question him.

"I'm so glad you came out," he said, rubbing his wrists.

"Tell us what happened," Skyler said.

"Some guy stuck a gun in my back and tied me up. Then he took your pizzas and used a dropper to put something liquid on them."

Cash shot a look at Jake. "Could be peanut oil."

Jake curled his hands into fists.

Skyler mumbled something before stepping out of earshot of the driver. Jake and Cash joined her.

"So it looks like the kidnapper came to the door with pizza right under our noses," she said.

"My fault." Cash frowned and stared into the distance. "I should have been more diligent. After all, he fits the build of the kidnapper. All I saw was a delivery guy."

"Don't beat yourself up," Skyler said. "That's what each of us would have seen if we answered the door."

Cash shook his head and continued staring. Jake understood the guilt Cash was feeling.

"Let it go," Jake said, yet knowing full well that if he was in Cash's shoes, he wouldn't have been able to do so. "Rachael's going to be fine."

"Right," Cash said, but there was no conviction in his voice.

Skyler dug out her phone. "I'll call this in and get some uniforms out here to search the neighborhood."

As she talked on the phone, sirens broke through the quiet.

Jake tipped his head in their direction. "That'll be the ambulance. I'm going in to check on Rachael."

In the entryway, he stomped the snow from his boots, then hurried to the dining room. He found Rachael sitting up next to Darcie, who was still monitoring Rachael's blood pressure and heart rate.

Darcie looked up. "She'll be fine, but she'll need to remain under observation in case another reaction occurs."

"It can come back?" Jake asked.

"Yes, with some people. Usually in twenty-four to forty-eight hours." Darcie changed her focus to Rachael. "Have you had a severe reaction like this before?"

Rachael nodded and lifted the mask. "It didn't return."

"I still insist on you going to the hospital to get checked out," Darcie said.

Jake waited for Rachael to argue, but she didn't speak.

"What did you find outside?" Darcie asked.

Jake told them about the driver. "He's fine, but he said the guy who tied him up put something liquid on the pizza. We're guessing peanut oil."

"How do you think he found me here?" Rachael asked.

"Simple," Skyler said as she walked into the room. "I suspect after seeing Jake at your house, he tracked him down. After all, it's no secret that the team lives here." She stepped closer, her gaze staying on Rachael. "What I'm more interested in learning right now is how he could know about your peanut allergy."

Jake could guess what Skyler was thinking—that this might be another indicator Rachael knew the kidnapper and was involved. He didn't want to embrace the same thought, but it was the easiest explanation for the guy knowing about her allergy.

Rachael sat up higher. "We post children's allergies in visible locations in our classrooms. I've included staff on the list so when parents bring in birthday treats, they're aware of all allergies in the center. My name and allergy would be listed in every classroom."

"The kidnapper could have seen it on either of his visits to the building," Jake added with relief.

Rachael nodded. "And when he broke into my house, he could have taken my EpiPen."

"But you checked your purse," Skyler said.

"I didn't actually look in the case." Rachael sighed. "I never even considered he would steal my EpiPen, so I only confirmed the case was in my purse."

Jake looked at Skyler. "That would mean our suspect's been thinking about poisoning Rachael since the break-in."

Skyler nodded. "Could be that his real purpose for the break-in was to steal the EpiPen, and the warning on the mirror was a distraction."

"The same thing could be true at the center." Rachael sat forward. "He needed to search for additional EpiPens and left the picture to cover up that break-in, too."

Skyler pondered the comment, then gave a firm nod. "Makes sense. After all, it wouldn't do any good to give you peanuts if you had an EpiPen handy."

Heavy boots sounded from the hallway, and Cash marched straight to Rachael. "This is all my fault. I should have paid more attention to the driver. I'm sorry."

"I don't blame you." She waved a hand. "Maybe if you describe him to me, it will help me remember his face."

"He had a sandy-brown beard and mustache. Long nose and tinted wire-framed glasses." Cash closed his eyes. "The tint kept me from seeing his eye color."

"I know the kidnapper didn't wear glasses," Rachael said. "But that's all I remember."

"He was likely wearing a disguise, or he wouldn't have shown his face," Jake said.

The mood in the room turned more somber, and they all remained still and unspeaking for a long, painful moment.

Skyler cleared her throat, breaking the quiet. "The good news in all of this is that Cash saw our suspect's face, and he can meet with a sketch artist."

"But if the suspect was disguised, how will that help?" Darcie asked.

"The sketch could provide enough detail to jog Rachael's memory."

"I'll try my best," she said.

Jake nodded. *But the bad news is the kidnapper upped the stakes to attempted murder.*

No matter how hard he tried to shake it, he knew it was the truth—and he needed to up his game to match the raised stakes.

* * *

After only an hour in the hospital, where the doctors had given Rachael Benadryl and monitored her condition, Jake drove her back to the firehouse. She'd agreed to hang out in the family room for a little longer so Darcie could keep an eye on her. Skyler joined them and was scurrying around the room, taking down decorations from her annual Christmas party for homeless families. She needed to make room for more personal decor like Christmas stockings for team members and their significant others, and she was also hanging homemade ornaments whittled by Brady.

Every few minutes she'd stop and clutch her stomach, showing them all that she was still having health issues. Jake considered saying something, but he saw Darcie watching her, and she eventually got up to join Skyler.

"Enough," Darcie said. "You're clearly not feeling well, and I'm taking you upstairs and putting you to bed."

Darcie pried a Santa figurine from Skyler's hand and shoved it at Jake. He took it, but didn't know the first thing about decorating, so he trailed behind them to ask where Skyler wanted him to put it.

At the bottom of the stairs, Darcie stopped. "Is your only symptom still nausea?"

"That, and I'm feeling more tired."

"Does the nausea still come and go?"

"Yes."

"Is there any chance you're pregnant?" Darcie asked.

Skyler's mouth fell open, and Jake stopped dead in his tracks. He knew with everyone on the team getting engaged or married recently that pregnancy was something to expect, but still, the thought took him by surprise.

"From the look on your face, it's possible." Darcie smiled.

Skyler blinked a few times. "It's not only possible, but very likely. Why didn't I see it?"

"Because as usual, you're letting an investigation take over."

Skyler kept blinking as if she couldn't believe the news. "I'll have to drive to the store to pick up a test."

"You go up and rest, and I'll run to the store for you."

Skyler grabbed Darcie's arm. "Make sure no one sees you, and promise me you won't tell anyone. I don't want Logan hearing about this from someone on the team."

"Don't worry. I can keep a secret."

Jake stepped back into the shadows, because he wanted Skyler to relax and not worry about anyone else knowing her news.

Once Skyler went upstairs and Darcie walked out the front door, Jake returned to the family room. Rachael had gotten up and was hanging stockings on brass holders at the fireplace. For years there had been only six stockings, but now, with all the significant others and Isabel, the number had doubled. Would there be a baby's stocking there next year?

Jake could easily imagine Logan and Skyler with a baby, standing in the glow of the fireplace. Sure, they'd likely move out of their condo at the firehouse and find a home of their own, but Jake suspected they'd still spend Christmas with the team. Or at least, he hoped they would.

And what about the others? When would they have children and move out? Would he be alone in this big old place that had seemed wonderful until right now?

Everything had changed so rapidly, and the thought of even more change speared his heart. He didn't want it to change. Didn't want the team to go their separate ways.

Then it hit him like a two-by-four upside the head. He

was jealous of Skyler and Logan's happiness. He'd never been jealous of the team's relationships, so why now?

Dumbfounded, he stared at Rachael.

Had she changed him in just a few days? Did he want a relationship with a woman, even with all the messiness and tremendous risk of getting hurt? Did he truly want that, or did it even matter what he wanted when she'd made it clear how she felt about him?

Rachael turned to retrieve another stocking from the table and caught his gaze. The fire glowed behind her, and she looked beautiful—so incredibly beautiful that he had to force himself not to cross over to her.

Because even if a relationship now seemed appealing, that was not an option for him. Not with the promise he'd once made to his family, and with so many people still needing his help.

Kelly's cries brought Rachael to a sitting position on the sofa in Jake's condo. Pam stepped out of the bedroom, jiggling a very fussy Kelly.

"Sorry," Pam said, looking exhausted. "I hate that she woke you."

"No problem. Do you need help?"

"I've got it." She dug through her diaper bag and held up a diaper. "This is the last one."

"We left the extra supplies in the entryway. I'll go grab some diapers." Rachael tugged an oversize sweater over her T-shirt and leggings and stepped into the hallway.

Thankfully, she didn't have any residual side effects from the allergy attack, except for being afraid it would happen again. She jogged down the stairs and dug through the large shopping bag for the pack of diapers they'd picked up on the way to the firehouse. She saw a light on in the family room and decided to investigate.

She found Jake standing at the lighted tree, his back to her. He was hanging the ornaments that Skyler had left behind. Rachael knew she should head back upstairs, but the homey scene in front of her kept her mesmerized.

Memories of her Christmases with Eli flitted through her mind. She missed their special times together. Missed being married. How wonderful life would be if she were in her own home right now, her husband standing at the tree before her and their child sleeping upstairs.

She hugged the diapers against her chest and sighed. She hadn't let herself dare to think of such a thing in a very long time. Not with the memory of that Christmas Eve four years ago that so often came to mind.

Would she ever regain her love of Christmas? She suddenly wanted to, but the vision of her and Eli after church on that last night together whisked away her hope.

She hadn't wanted him to go out for the ice cream. In fact, she didn't ask and had gone to bed, but the craving for something cold wouldn't let up. So she got up, searched the freezer and even chewed on ice cubes.

Eli joined her and joked about her craving. He'd insisted on running to the convenience store. As he stood by the door, he turned, that sweet smile he had just for her crossing his face. He blew her a kiss, winked and said he'd be home in a flash.

He didn't come home. Not in a flash. Not ever.

Instead, a police officer came to the door. The shock of his news brought her to her knees, her hand cupping her belly to protect their baby as she fell. She called her friend Annie, who sat with her into the wee hours of the night as Rachael tried to forget her loss for just a moment to eat so she could nourish the baby, and try to sleep.

She'd managed a few bites and a few hours of sleep. Then time moved on, and she didn't. She would look at Eli's clothes, his sweaters, his laundry in the basket, and wonder what she should do with that. How did she go on alone?

Then, a month later, she remembered with painful clarity waking in the night with cramps and bleeding. Annie racing her to the hospital. Miscarrying before morning. The pain had swallowed her whole, and she could do nothing more than grieve.

The memories now brought the pain back to life, fresh and intense, but something else was there, too. The desire for a family. It was something she hadn't dared to admit to herself since Eli had died and she'd lost the baby.

Seeing Jake like this, with her feelings for him growing, proved that she wanted more—but it didn't matter. She turned her back and marched up the stairs.

Her only family would be the ones at the center. They needed her help, and even now, as she knew she wanted more, she also knew she didn't deserve it.

TEN

The sun shone bright the next morning on Jake's drive to visit Pam's parents in Tigard. Jake had dropped Pam off at work, with Rachael babysitting Kelly. Jake reluctantly left Rachael under Cash's watchful eye. It wasn't that Jake no longer trusted Cash after the peanut incident—that could have happened to anyone—but Jake simply didn't want to leave her care to anyone else. That should have told him something about the feelings he was developing for her, but he refused to dwell on it.

He parked in front of a small bungalow and climbed out. Two cars sat in the driveway, which didn't fit with Skyler's research. She'd said the mother's shift ended at seven and the dad started at six, meaning only the mother should have been home right now. It was something Jake had been counting on, as in his experience, women were often more forthcoming than men.

He knocked on the door and unclipped his badge from his belt.

Mrs. Baldwin answered. "Can I help you?"

"I'm Deputy Jake Marsh, Mrs. Baldwin," he said, displaying his badge for her.

She arched a brow and planted her feet. "It's Pam, isn't it? You've come to tell us she's finally overdosed."

"No," Jake said quickly. "Pam is fine. In fact, she's more than fine. She's doing great." He added the last bit because, surprisingly, he'd developed a fondness for Pam, and he was proud of her success and wished these parents would be, too. Though, to be fair, he hadn't witnessed her volatile history with drugs as her parents had.

Mrs. Baldwin crossed her arms. "So what is it, then?"

"Do you mind if I come in? I have a few questions for you."

"Regarding?"

"Pam."

"I knew it had to be about her. It's the only time we ever get visits from the cops." She sounded bitter, but she led him into a small dining room with a round wooden table, where Mr. Baldwin was drinking a cup of coffee, a newspaper folded in front of him. Short and squat, he had a full head of black hair with gray at the temples. He was a few inches shorter, and many inches wider, than the kidnapper as he'd been described.

"This here's Deputy Marsh," Mrs. Baldwin said. "It's something about Pam."

"Of course it is." Mr. Baldwin frowned and gestured at a vacant chair.

Jake sat. "My coworker, Detective Skyler Hunter, talked to you yesterday about Pam."

"That's right."

"You said neither of you had heard from or spoken to her in years."

"Also true," Mrs. Baldwin said, dropping into a chair by her husband.

"How did you learn about Kelly, then?"

"Got a call from Pam's social worker," Mr. Baldwin said. "She needed to verify information on Pam, and she mentioned the baby." He shook his head.

"Looks like you don't approve of Kelly."

He crossed his arms. "I don't. Not of having a baby out of wedlock, but mostly I don't think Pam will be a very good mother."

"Not if her history is any indication," Mrs. Baldwin added.

"Do you think you'd be better at raising Kelly?"

"Of course we would!" Mrs. Baldwin exclaimed.

Jake stared at Mr. Baldwin. Though he wasn't the right build for the kidnapper, he could have hired the man. "Suppose you tell me where you were at six on Monday morning."

"At work."

"Do you work the same shift every day?"

"Six until three. Monday through Friday."

"And yet you're home now."

"I'm taking a sick day." He faked a cough.

"Your supervisor can vouch for you for today and the other morning?"

He nodded.

Jake pulled out a notepad and slid it across the table with a pen. "Write down his contact information."

"Why do you want to know where he was?" Mrs. Baldwin asked.

"Someone tried to abduct Kelly from her child care center."

Mr. Baldwin shot to his feet. "And you think I might have done that? You're nuts."

"Still, I'll need your supervisor's contact information, and I'll also need to know where you were yesterday around four thirty."

"Right here. Eating an early dinner before watching TV."

"Can anyone vouch for you?"

"We were eating together," Mrs. Baldwin offered, sounding far less belligerent. Jake believed her.

Mr. Baldwin scribbled his work information on the page, then stood, glaring at Jake. "Is that all you need?"

"For now." Jake stood, too, and picked up his notepad. "You can expect to hear from me again if this doesn't check out."

The couple exchanged a look, but it vanished as quickly as it had appeared. Mrs. Baldwin showed him to the door.

"Anything else you'd like to tell me?" Jake asked her from the porch, hoping that she might share more now that they were out of Mr. Baldwin's hearing.

She seemed to ponder for a moment before shaking her head and shutting the door in his face.

Jake didn't want to waste any time, so the moment he settled in his truck, he dialed Mr. Baldwin's place of employment. When his supervisor came on the line and told Jake that Mr. Baldwin had showed up two hours late on Monday morning without an explanation, Jake's mouth almost hit his chest. Jake thanked the supervisor and strode back to the house.

He pounded on the door, but no one answered. Jake wasn't going to let them get away with not talking to him, so he parked himself on the porch and waited.

An hour later, Mr. Baldwin poked his head out the door. "We're through talking to you until our lawyer is present."

Jake doubted the family had a lawyer on retainer, and figured Mr. Baldwin had simply heard the lawyer threat many times on TV. Either way, it didn't matter. The man wasn't going to talk, and Jake was wasting his time trying to get him to speak.

The good news was that if Pam's father really did believe he needed a lawyer, he likely had something to hide.

Once Jake told Skyler about the conversation, she would insist on bringing him down to the station and placing him in an interrogation room, which often encouraged suspects to talk.

Jake drove back to the firehouse and located Skyler in the office on the main floor. She still looked pale and, if possible, greener than yesterday. Since he knew the probable reason now, he chose not to mention it.

He recounted the information he'd learned at the Baldwin residence. "As you said, Pam's father isn't the right build for the kidnapper, but they're hiding something. Perhaps he skipped work so the real kidnapper could hand Kelly over to him."

Skyler nodded. "I'll be glad to contact their lawyer, if they really do have one. Then we'll see how tough this guy is. And I'll have the techs pull video feeds from the general area around their home to see if we can catch him in his car that morning."

"You think they're involved?"

"First rule of investigation. Don't form any opinions that facts don't support."

Jake eyed her. "But you formed an opinion on Rachael."

"Honestly, I haven't. I just said we have to keep an open mind in case we discover she's involved. Maybe I hit it a little hard, but I thought I needed to balance you out, as you've gone completely in the opposite direction."

"True," he said. "And I won't apologize for it. Rachael needs someone in her corner."

Skyler gathered her papers. "Problem is, you want more than to be in her corner. You want to invade her whole life."

Jake arched a brow, but didn't bother arguing. After his behavior of late, he couldn't deny the obvious. It was best for him just to move on.

"Did you find Pam's past boyfriends?" he asked.

Skyler came to her feet. "Actually, we just got a lead on the whereabouts of Hal Ladell. He hangs out in an abandoned building on the north side, and I'm heading over to talk to him."

"Do you think he could have done this?"

She shrugged. "Both guys have records. The height and weight for both of them are in line with the kidnapper's build."

"Do you think it's of any value to show their mug shots to Rachael?"

"Couldn't hurt."

"I'll take care of that, then."

She nodded.

"Have you checked for stolen cars matching the one the suspect fled from Francie's apartment in?" he asked.

She shook her head. "You think it was stolen?"

He shrugged. "If I was going to try to kidnap a baby, I wouldn't want to use my personal vehicle."

"Good point."

"I'll check the database and see what I can come up with."

"You should know I've reviewed traffic cam footage near the center for Monday morning. No sign of that Honda." She stepped from the room, pausing to grab the doorjamb for a second.

Jake couldn't imagine what it felt like to be nauseated every day. Sure, having a baby was a great reward, but still, feeling like you were going to be sick all the time had to be taxing.

He sat behind the computer and logged in to the county's database to plug in the make and model of the Honda. He scrolled down the most recent log and came upon two Accords stolen in the last month. One of the reports was dated three days ago, and the Portland Police Bureau had handled the call.

Jake dialed the detective in charge of the case and explained his need for information. The detective agreed to email a copy of the stolen vehicle report. Jake hung up and waited for his email account to display a new message. When it did, he clicked on the file and located the address where the car was stolen, then sat back to think.

He seemed to be on target with the stolen vehicle hunch, so maybe the guy had used the car to steal the ketamine, too. A vet's office would be a far easier target than a medical facility, and the thief could have found the car near the vet's office.

Jake plugged the car owner's address into a map program and searched for veterinarians, then also added doctors' offices and hospitals in a five-mile radius.

The map returned a few results, but Jake focused on a veterinary clinic located on a corner very close to the car theft address. Even more important, the address was near Mr. Baldwin's job.

Jake grabbed the phone and dialed the PPB detective again.

"Any chance there was a burglary in a veterinarian's office in the same area where the car was stolen?" Jake asked.

"Hold on," the detective said.

Time ticked by, and Jake tapped his finger on the desk.

"Yeah, man. The Pet Spot, the same night."

"Can you transfer me to the detective who worked the case?"

"Yeah. Hold on again."

Jake was soon transferred to the other detective. Jake identified himself. "What can you tell me about the break-in at The Pet Spot?"

"They were after drugs, what else? Ketamine, to be specific."

Jake explained how ketamine fit into his investigation. "I was hoping I could take a look at your report and the evidence."

"Sure, man. Since it involved drugs, we called out forensics. They lifted evidence, but none of it panned out. Looks like the items we recovered were from the normal course of doing business."

Jake wouldn't have made such an assumption. "When can I stop by to look at the report and evidence?"

"I'll be out of the office all day, but I can have the information waiting for you tomorrow morning."

They scheduled a time, and Jake hung up. He entered the vet's address into the map program and scanned the surrounding businesses. A halfway house popped up just down the block.

Jake sat back, his mind whirring.

Could Sid Cooper, Pam's other ex, have moved to the house? Was he behind the kidnapping?

Maybe.

Jake texted Skyler to tell her about his lead. Ideally she would be able to obtain a list of the halfway house residents, and Sid Cooper's name would be on it.

At The Pet Spot, Rachael stood near a wall filled with crates holding recuperating dogs and cats. She and Jake were on their way to the center and he'd wanted to stop in on the way. With the way the vet kept watching her, she wished they'd headed straight to the center.

A tall man in his thirties with tousled dishwater-blond hair and a nose that reminded her of a mini pig snout, the vet locked his eyes on her. She suspected he watched her because he could feel her discomfort with the pets, who were clamoring to be released. She'd never been an animal person. Not because she didn't like them. She'd simply had no exposure to them as a child, as her mother had been allergic.

"That's where I know you from!" he exclaimed. "I saw you on the news. Oh, man, I'm sorry. That must have been horrible." His expression turned suspicious. "You aren't… I mean, the reporter… He said you were involved. But you couldn't be, right? You're here with the police." He shot a look at Jake.

"Sometimes reporters get things wrong," Jake replied.

Rachael didn't like his vague answer. He could have said she wasn't involved and cleared her name, but he didn't.

"Gotcha," the vet said, but he kept glancing at Rachael like she had two heads.

She should have been thankful, she supposed, as it took her mind off the mug shots Jake had shown her before they'd left the house. She didn't recognize either Sid or Hal, but they were both mean-looking guys, and after seeing their rap sheets, she thought either one could have tried to kidnap little Kelly.

"This is where we keep our meds locked up." The vet pointed at a steel cabinet on the far wall. "That's not the actual cabinet, though. The burglar destroyed the other one, so I had to replace it."

Jake looked from the window to the cabinet and back again. Then his gaze roamed over the room. Rachael wished she could read his thoughts. Not only now, but all the time. Especially when it came to her. Or maybe she didn't want to know what he thought, because it might make her consider things she wasn't ready for.

Jake pointed at the far wall and a security camera

mounted near the ceiling. "Did the detective pull your video feed?"

The vet nodded. "But I made copies of the files for my insurance company. You're welcome to look at them if you'd like."

Jake glanced at his watch. "We have an appointment in a few minutes. Could you email them to me?"

"Sure."

Jake handed his business card to the vet. "You've been most helpful."

"Are you kidding?" The vet laughed. "I'll do anything I can to find this guy. Ketamine isn't something that should be handled without a medical license." The vet changed his focus to Rachael. "I'm sorry if he used drugs stolen from my practice to inject you. I've installed a top-of-the-line security system, so it shouldn't happen again."

"You have nothing to be sorry for," Rachael assured him.

Jake tapped his watch. "We should get going."

"Thank you again," Rachael said, and followed Jake out to his truck.

She settled in and buckled her seat belt. "Except for the fact that the vet thought I was a criminal, he seemed to be a nice guy."

Jake started the car and glanced at her. "He's a victim in all of this, just like you."

She was so surprised to hear him say he believed she was a victim that she stared at him for a minute. "So you've finally decided I'm not involved."

"I never really believed you were, but honestly if I *had* thought you were guilty, as I got to know you, I'd have let that go. You're conscientious and caring about the families you work with. You'd never hurt them. Not a single one of them. That's clear."

His admission warmed her heart more than she wanted to admit. "I'm glad you figured that out."

"Why?" he asked.

"Why what?"

"Why do you devote so much of yourself to your families? I mean, as far as I can see, you don't have much of a life outside the center."

"I want it that way." She wondered how much to tell him about her past and decided to reiterate what she'd already told him. "When I was struggling to go on after Eli died, God showed me that helping these needy families was to be my path in life."

"And you think that helping them means you have to spend your life alone?"

"Don't you think the same thing? People need us, and we have to give them our all."

He nodded, but his forehead creased, and he didn't seem to believe it.

She wanted to pursue the conversation further, but she'd vowed to keep things professional—and asking why he chose to be alone and not have a personal life was as unprofessional as it got.

The licensing rep was round and short, and wore a serious pucker. Jake could tell she was treating her visit to Rachael's center solemnly, and if her sour look gave any indication of her willingness to lift the suspension, it wouldn't happen. In fact, she looked so terse, Jake hated to leave Rachael alone in the office with her. But as a law enforcement officer, he was a reminder of the severity of the problem, so he took his iPad to the staff lounge and sank down into a comfy sofa.

He opened his iPad case, but the uneasy look on Rachael's face kept distracting him from his email. He suspected Rachael thought that losing her center was similar to losing a child. Her suffering continued to multiply, and it made Jake mad that God didn't intervene and help her out.

Why? he asked. *Why let this happen?*

Jake had asked the same question for years after his family had died. A question he still asked when he saw someone needlessly suffering, as he often witnessed on the job. He never received a satisfactory answer, so he'd stopped expecting one.

After all, why try to maintain a relationship with God if He never answered?

At least that's how he'd felt for years, but Rachael's continued faith in the wake of losing her husband made Jake want to revisit this issue and try to understand God's purpose in suffering. Over the years, Jake had read or heard that God used suffering to make people stronger. All it seemed to do for him was make him worry more about putting himself in a position where he could lose people he cared about—but there had to be more to it, right?

On his iPad, he logged in to an online Bible program and searched for *worry*. The first verse that came up was Matthew 6:34:

Therefore do not worry about tomorrow, for tomorrow will worry about itself. Each day has enough trouble of its own.

"Isn't that the truth?" he mumbled, thinking about the last few days.

He could never have predicted the problems he and Rachael had encountered. Nor could he have predicted that in such a short time he would actually be thinking that life held more than he'd been experiencing. So maybe God was talking to him. Telling him to take each day as it came and stop thinking God should change his situation. To consider why God allowed him to remain in these difficult situations.

His iPad signaled the receipt of an email. Could be from the vet. He navigated to the email and discovered the vet had indeed sent the promised videos.

Jake played the first one date-stamped 2:00 a.m. Friday night. A masked man fitting the build of Kelly's kidnapper smashed the window, glass flying in all directions. He then shimmied through the opening and crossed the room to raid the medicine cabinet before leaving the same way he'd entered.

Jake tapped the link for outside cameras that captured the suspect rushing across the parking lot to the street, but the range didn't extend far enough to show the vehicle he departed in.

Jake emailed Skyler and asked her to look at traffic cam footage for the Accord in the surrounding area.

He closed his iPad case, disappointed that he hadn't learned anything new, but he still had hope for the physical evidence secured at the PPB property room.

Raised voices drifted from the office, grabbing his attention.

Was Rachael arguing with her rep? Odd. Rachael wanted the visit to go well and arguing was counterproductive.

Perhaps he could help. He stepped into the hallway and listened.

"I don't understand," Rachael said. "I'll write a letter indicating my intent to comply with your corrective actions, so why don't you think the suspension will be lifted?"

"It very well might be, but I know the committee will look more favorably upon your request if the kidnapper has been caught. I realize this has nothing to do with your willingness to comply with the regulations, and in all honesty, it's none of their business if the kidnapper is still at large. They shouldn't let it color their decision, but I know they'd rest easier if the threat was no longer valid."

"As I mentioned earlier, the police believe the kidnapping is specific to Kelly and the other children aren't in danger. What if I asked to have the suspension lifted but agreed not to let Kelly return until the kidnapper is caught?"

"Are the police one hundred percent sure?"

"No. Not one hundred percent."

"Then I'm going to suggest again that you wait to ask for the suspension to be lifted," Yolanda said. "But it's your decision, and you should do what you think is best. You're one of the most caring and diligent providers I know, Rachael, and I only want to give you the best chance to succeed."

Jake thought Rachael would take Yolanda's advice and wait to request the suspension be lifted. He also suspected that she'd be upset, and he hoped he could find a way to help her handle another setback.

They stepped into the hallway, and Jake turned his attention to a parent bulletin board while Rachael bid Yolanda goodbye.

He saw a flyer for a fund-raiser scheduled that evening for a group called Children at Risk—CAR for short. According to the flyer, the group helped low-income parents secure quality child and health care and helped provide for their everyday living needs. It made perfect sense that Rachael supported such a cause but no sense that she hadn't mentioned she was the scheduled guest speaker for tonight.

When the door closed, he joined her in the foyer. "I overheard the end of your conversation with Yolanda. Are you going to wait to ask to have the suspension repealed?"

She peered up at him. "It seems like the prudent thing to do."

"I know this is another setback for you. Is there anything I can do?"

"Find the kidnapper."

He kept failing her, reminding him of how he'd let down his family. "I'll meet with the team and see if we can do better."

"No, no. I wasn't criticizing. I know you're doing your very best and I'm blessed to have you and your team working this investigation and looking out for my safety."

"Speaking of safety, I noticed a flyer." He pointed at the parent board. "There's a fund-raiser tonight, and you're the speaker?"

"Oh, no." She clamped a hand over her mouth. "With everything going on, I forgot all about it." She dropped her hand. "We'll have to stop by my house for my dress."

He gaped at her. "You're still planning on going?"

"Yes, of course. Why wouldn't I?"

"The kidnapper is getting more desperate, and he's escalating. You never know what he might try. You could be in extreme danger traveling to and from the event, or even at the event."

"But I have to go. I can't let down the children who will benefit from the funds raised tonight. Also, the founders of CAR are good friends of mine, and they're counting on me. I won't disappoint them."

"I'd rather you didn't go."

She stepped closer and gazed into his eyes. "Please, Jake. You know how much helping at-risk parents means to me. Isn't there a way I can attend and minimize the danger to myself and others?"

He stepped back, because when she looked at him with pleading eyes, he wanted to give her anything her heart desired, and giving in without proper thought would be a big mistake.

He thought about the venue where they would hold the fund-raiser. Could he keep her safe there? Maybe.

"From what I know of the venue, it could be manageable. But I'll need to visit the place this afternoon and develop a security plan with the team before I'll agree to let you go."

"You do know I could just drive myself there."

"Would you?" he asked, hating that the idea of how her going against his wishes made him feel sick inside.

"No." She smiled softly. "I'll just keep pestering you until you say yes."

"Pester all you want, but I won't agree unless it's safe."

She studied him intently, and he felt like her gaze laid bare all of his inner thoughts and fears of letting others down. Of failing to be there when others needed him.

"This goes back to losing your family, right?" she asked. "You're overly cautious because of that, I mean."

He could dodge her question and keep from admitting how his loss lingered and how he allowed it to run his life, but why? She'd figured it out anyway so he nodded.

She sighed. "I understand—at least, kind of. You're trying to protect people from physical harm. For me, it's emotional harm. After losing Eli, I have to protect my heart." She laughed nervously. "That probably doesn't make any sense to you."

"It does," he said.

She eyed him again.

He might have let her know how losing his family continued to direct his life, but he didn't want her to know how much the chance of her getting hurt affected his emotional health. "We should get going so I have time to check out the venue and talk to the rest of my team."

"Thank you." She suddenly wound her arms around his neck and hugged him hard. "I'm so grateful for your help."

Stunned, he settled his hands at her waist. He wasn't sure how to react. Especially when her arms tightened and she pulled him even closer.

She smelled like the air after a fresh rain, and she was warm and soft in his arms. A warmth that he'd never known before raced through his veins and flooded his heart. He crushed her to him and held on as if she was a life preserver. She must have felt the change in him as she planted her palms against his chest and pushed back.

"Sorry," she said and looked away. "I was out of line."

"No problem," he replied, though she hadn't been out of line. It was him—all him—letting the awareness of how wonderful it would be to have a woman like her in his life sway his resolve.

ELEVEN

Rachael glanced around the large ballroom of the down-town Portland hotel. After the week she'd experienced, she didn't feel much like attending the fund-raiser, but she never backed down from a commitment. She would simply make the best of things. She wished Pam could have accompanied them as originally planned, but Pam wanted to avoid having to answer endless questions about the kidnapping. Rachael didn't blame her, so they'd left her in Jake's condo with Cash and Brady in charge of protecting her and Kelly.

The room was decorated for Christmas in cool blues and silvers, everything sparkling in the bright spotlights. Rachael thought of the firehouse, the lights turned down low, the tree lit by multicolor lights and the fireplace glowing and warming up the room. This room didn't hold a candle to Detective Hunter's decorating efforts. Rachael found this space to be cold and uninviting, whereas the firehouse she could easily imagine calling home. Calling Jake's friends her own.

How had she gotten so attached to the FRS, and even to Detective Hunter? She'd tried hard not to, but…

She sighed.

"Is everything okay?" Jake asked, standing next to her.

"Fine," she said and shrugged out of her jacket.

He took her coat and his gaze roved over her. "Wow. You look amazing."

He'd seen her dress when he'd picked it up at her house, but she'd dressed and put her coat on in his condo, so he hadn't seen her wearing it until now.

His gaze lifted to her face and held. "Your dress is even more spectacular than it was on the hanger."

She was powerless to look away.

No. Oh. No.

She'd been concerned about getting close to the FRS, but what about Jake? She'd let him into a place in her heart that had been vacant for a very long time. Worse yet, she liked the warm feelings instead of the emptiness. Liked it too much. But that didn't mean she was ready to embrace it, or him, again.

"Thanks again for picking it up from my house," she said quickly, then looked away so he wouldn't see how much his simple compliment impacted her.

"I'll go check the coats." He took them to the counter, and while he arranged for a number, she searched the room for William and Gloria.

Rachael still couldn't believe she'd bonded with the founders of CAR. Wealthy, philanthropic socialites, they lived in a world Rachael had never inhabited, but once they'd gotten to know each other, they'd discovered their hearts were in the same place. And both William and Gloria had lost spouses before they'd found each other. They understood Rachael's grief and didn't push her toward finding another mate the way others did.

"Should we go in?" Jake asked, coming up behind her.

She nodded. His black suit and crisp white shirt made him look undeniably handsome. The suit appeared custom-made, but he kept fidgeting with his tie and telling her that he didn't wear suits often. As they stepped into the room, he remained close by her side. They had taken only a few steps when his stomach rumbled.

"Sorry." He grinned. "Guess you can't take me out in public."

She turned to glance up at him, and her heart did a little flip-flop at his endearing smile.

"I could use something to eat before my speech, too." She gestured at the buffet tables set up in front of a wall of windows overlooking the river. "Let's grab a plate."

He indicated she should precede him, but his gaze continued to rove over the room. He seemed worried about her safety and wasn't going to let down his guard. Yet one more reason to like the guy.

She stepped up to the white-draped table with blue and silver glittery balls lying atop greenery that ran the table length. Miniature pine trees wrapped in gauzy white and blue ribbon sat in the middle and at each end of the table. White plates and sparkling silverware completed the decor.

Rachael took a plate and loaded it with appetizers, salad and roast beef. Jake skipped the salad and piled the beef high on his plate. The amount of food he'd taken compared to what Eli used to eat took her by surprise, but Jake was a good six inches taller and thirty pounds heavier than Eli, most of it muscle.

What was she doing comparing the two of them? It wasn't like she planned for Jake to become a part of her life as Eli had been.

Plate in hand, Jake searched the room, this time looking like he sought an open table. She wanted to sit next to the window and look out over the river, but he gestured at a round table in the corner, far away from the windows. "That's a perfect spot."

She assumed he meant perfect for protecting her, because it wasn't perfect for socializing or for the scenery. Still, before they'd left the firehouse, she'd promised to follow his directions, so she picked up a glass of punch and stepped toward the table.

"Rachael," Ursula Ingram, CAR's program manager, called out, bringing Rachael to a stop as the tall brunette joined her.

"How are Pam and Kelly doing?" Ursula asked.

"As well as can be expected," Rachael replied.

"I called Pam and left a message, but when she didn't return my call, I worried that she might have slipped and started using again."

"No, she's holding her own."

"Good." Ursula changed her focus to Jake.

Rachael introduced Ursula and told her about Jake's role in stopping the kidnapping.

"You're a hero, then." She smiled up at him. "Perhaps we should introduce you after Rachael's speech so CAR's members can thank you properly."

Jake cringed. "That's not necessary."

"But it would be nice."

"Honestly, it might be for you all, but not for me."

"A hero who is modest." Ursula turned her attention to Rachael. "And I see that he's not wearing a wedding ring."

Heat rushed up Rachael's neck. "Our food is getting cold. I'll check in with you when it's time for my speech."

She stepped off, and Jake walked by her side.

"Sorry about the wedding ring thing," she said. "Ursula's always trying to fix me up and get me married off. Which is really weird, as she lost her husband twenty years ago and never remarried."

They continued on, but several other supporters stopped her to ask about Pam and Kelly.

"Seems like everyone is concerned about them," Jake said as they neared the table. "Is that concern common for all of the people CAR supports?"

"Yes, but even more so for Pam, as she represents the success we strive for in every person we help. The members have a vested interest in seeing her continue to succeed."

"All of the members take a personal interest, then, even the leaders?"

"William and Gloria used to be the best example of that, but as the organization has grown, they've had to hand off their administrative duties to Ursula. They work in a fund-raising and PR capacity now, so they aren't intimately involved in the participants' lives."

"They sound like great people."

"They are," Rachael said. "William has been so successful with the drug rehab portion of the program that he's expanded it to include people in the inner circle of the parents we help."

"Isn't that a little out of your group's mission statement?"

"Not really. Many of the women in the program got involved with drugs due to their relationships. If we can assist these other people, too, it keeps our clients away from drugs and helps them stay clean."

At their table, Jake set down his food, then pulled out a chair for her before taking the seat next to her. She would have liked to look at him during dinner, though she knew it wasn't a good idea, but he'd chosen for both of them to sit with their backs to the wall and facing the crowd. Safety, she supposed again, but it felt awkward. She turned her attention to her food and spread hummus on a thick pita chip. Jake dug into his beef, but he kept raising his head and watching the action in front of them. She wished he could simply sit back and enjoy the night instead of spending every moment worried about her safety.

"I hate that you have to work tonight." She took a bite of the freshly made hummus, the adobo chilies used for seasoning giving the hummus a bite.

"No worries. I'm used to it."

"Yes, you're very good at working," she said, but wished she hadn't when he narrowed his gaze.

"Then we're in the same boat, right?" He forked another bite of food and returned his gaze to the crowd.

She nodded, but the thought made her sadder than she'd been in a very long time. Here they were, clearly interested in each other, and yet they allowed their pasts to define them.

What would happen if they changed? Would they pursue this interest between them? Did it matter, as she didn't see change coming her way anytime soon, if ever?

They finished their meals in silence, and when Rachael finally spotted William, she got up to speak with him.

"Not so fast." Jake rested his hand on her arm.

"Sorry. I forgot I need to clear everything with you."

Though her comment had been sincere, he frowned as he escorted her across the room.

In his midforties, William was tall and thin and smelled of peppermint. He wore a tailored black tuxedo, white pleated shirt and black tie. His hair was pale blond, his gaze warm and friendly.

"Rachael," he said, opening his arms to give her a brief hug.

When he released her, she introduced Jake.

"Excuse us, please," William said to the others and tugged her off to the side. "Is he here on official business?"

"Sort of." Rachael explained the events of the last few days.

William took a step closer. "Gloria and I heard about the awful ordeal at your center, but I had no idea it continued to be a problem."

He shook his head, and his eyes creased. The threat to Kelly and her center had obviously impacted him.

"I wish there was something Gloria and I could do to help."

"Where is Gloria?" Rachael asked.

"At home sick, I'm afraid."

"She must really not feel well if she's missing a CAR event."

William nodded. "She does cherish her role in CAR."

"Role." Rachael laughed. "You're the founders. Don't be so modest."

He waved off her comment.

Rachael wouldn't embarrass him by belaboring the point. "I'll give Gloria a call tomorrow to check in on her."

"That's most kind of you," William said, but his attention had drifted to a nearby power couple. "I need to talk to the Grangers. They've got more money than they know what to do with, and I've been trying to get them to participate in another fund-raiser." He squeezed Rachael's arm. "If they agree to a donation tonight, you can expect a call from my assistant Thad in the next few days."

"Thad? What happened to Charles?" she asked, thinking about the young man she'd met just a few weeks ago when she'd visited William at CAR's offices.

A smile radiated from his face. "Charles graduated

from our program and got a new job. I'm grooming Thad for the same thing."

Rachael squeezed his hand. "Congratulations on another successful rehab."

"Charles is the one who needs congratulating. Not me. He's done all the hard work to get sober. Now if only Thad takes the same route." He looked at the Grangers again. "I really have to talk to them before they leave. Excuse me."

After William departed, Rachael tried to cross the room to the dais but was stopped by Olin and Lucy Kempner, a stylish couple in their midthirties. She introduced Jake.

"How is Pam holding up?" Lucy asked, just as so many others had that evening.

Rachael explained the situation.

"I wish I could talk to her to make sure she really is staying sober, but she's not answering her phone." Lucy clenched her hands, and Olin worked the muscles in his jaw. They were both likely thinking about Olin's past drug problem and the possibility that he could relapse someday, too.

"Pam is good, trust me. She just needs a bit of privacy right now," Rachael said, then moved them on to a discussion of an upcoming food drive they were both working on.

As usual, Lucy and Olin's enthusiasm for the cause rang through their voices and Rachael got caught up in the discussion, forgetting Jake was standing there until he tapped her arm.

He pointed across the room at the dais. "Ursula is waving you down."

"Sorry, we'll have to catch up later," Rachael told the couple and excused herself.

"The Kempners sound like they're quite involved in the program," Jake said as they started across the room.

Rachael thought about their struggles in recent years, and she couldn't help but frown.

"Did I say something wrong?" Jake asked.

"No, it's just that they've been through so much, and it's looking like Lucy might make things worse for them again."

"Okay, now you've made me curious, and you have to explain."

"They'd tried for years to have a child and spent all of their money on in vitro fertilization. The stress of trying to have a baby overwhelmed Olin, and he turned to drugs to escape. He lost his job, and they had to file for bankruptcy. They're just now trying to get back on their feet, but I know Lucy hasn't given up on having a child, and I worry that they'll head back down that same path of destruction."

Jake's eyes widened, and she could almost see suspicions running through his head.

"Now, wait," she said. "Just because they aren't able to have children and don't have the money for additional in vitro doesn't mean they tried to take Kelly."

"He's the right size for the kidnapper."

"But wouldn't seeing him tonight bring back my memory?"

"Not if it's gone permanently, which I'm beginning to think is the case after these last few days of you trying so hard to remember."

"I suppose," she said, sounding disappointed.

"Do the Kempners have a personal relationship with Pam, so they might have gotten to know Kelly better?"

"I think Lucy babysat for Kelly."

"Then Lucy needs to go on our suspect list."

Rachael sighed. "You know I hate this, right? It's so unfair to take a woman who has already suffered, and then accuse her of something like this."

"We won't accuse her of anything, but we will talk to her."

He was technically correct, but Rachael thought the Kempners would feel as if he was pointing the finger at them. Still, she supposed there was no way around it.

She gestured at Ursula, whose waving had turned frantic. "It's time for my speech."

His frown remaining, Jake escorted Rachael though the crowd. She gave what she hoped was an impassioned speech about how God implores people to help the less fortunate, and as she made the rounds of the room after she'd finished speaking, the warm response from CAR members told her she'd touched their hearts.

Her mouth dry, she led Jake to the punch bowl by the window.

"Look, more snow!" She squealed like a little child before she could control her enthusiasm. She pointed out the window, and people standing nearby caught sight of the snow. With it being a rare occurrence in the Portland area, they rushed to the window to peer outside.

"Won't be long before people leave to avoid the slippery roads and hills," Jake said. "We should get going before them, so I can keep a better eye out for your safety."

"And maybe get back to the firehouse soon enough to play in the snow."

Jake gaped at her.

Her childlike suggestion shocked him as much as it did her. She hadn't felt this lighthearted in a long time. Maybe the success of her speech had brought the change, but if she faced the truth, she'd have to admit that the man standing next to her had more to do with the changes in her emotions than anything else.

He urged her toward the coat check stand. "If there's any accumulation, the entire team will be outside by the time we get home."

He helped her into her coat, then put his arm around her waist and drew her tight against his body. She doubted he had to hold her this close for security's sake, but she had to admit she liked it and didn't pull away. They stepped into the parking garage, and a gust of wind pummeled them. She snuggled even closer and saw him smile.

The night had been so enjoyable that she could easily imagine it as a date, and she found that she didn't mind that idea, either.

They rounded the corner to the car, and she spotted a vagrant huddled by a post. He'd shoved his hands into his pockets and had propped a sign in his lap saying he was hungry. His head was covered with a frayed hood, his gaze looking down.

Rachael couldn't walk past the man and not offer him some money. She inched away from Jake and grabbed the emergency cash she always carried in her coat pocket. "It'll just take a minute."

"I don't think…" Jake said, but by the time he spoke, she was already halfway across the space.

She heard rushing footsteps behind her, and she turned to see if Jake was upset that she hadn't checked with him first.

"Gun!" he suddenly shouted, and launched himself through the air to wrap his powerful arms around her and tackle her to the ground.

A gunshot exploded from the area of the homeless man.

The sound echoed through the space as they slammed into the concrete, and she feared the next shot, if there was one, would pierce Jake's back and end his life.

TWELVE

Jake cocooned Rachael in his arms and took the brunt of the fall on his shoulder. Pain razored through his body. He ignored it and immediately rolled to cover Rachael.

Another shot rang through the air and a bullet slammed into his back, the force driving him into her. He'd chosen to wear a Kevlar vest under his dress shirt, not the heavy-duty combat vest he'd been wearing when the deputy shot him at Rachael's center, and the pain of the impact took his breath away. He tried to suck in deep breaths as he heard footsteps racing away from them and receding into the background.

Jake wanted to go after this guy, but he wasn't about to leave Rachael alone and unprotected. Up the incline, the shrill beep of a car alarm cut through the space. Then a door slammed and an engine roared. Wheels squealed on the concrete, and Jake knew the vehicle barreled down the ramp toward them.

He dug deep for strength that he still hadn't recovered, and rolled them both to a protected spot. Tires crunched over the concrete mere inches from his head. He tucked Rachael closer, squeezing her as tightly against his body as possible, then craned his neck to see the car.

"Same vehicle as the one outside Francie's apartment,"

he said and strained to catch the license plate. He could make out the first three digits, and they matched the car that had been stolen near the vet's office, so it added credence to that lead.

He lay there for a few minutes, cradling Rachael to be sure the shooter didn't return and open fire.

"Can we get up?" she asked, her voice shivery and timid.

"Sorry," he replied. "Not yet."

"Can you at least let go a little bit so I can breathe?"

"Yeah, sure. Sorry." He released her and dug out his phone to call dispatch to put out an alert on the vehicle and to notify Skyler of the incident.

When he finished his call and hadn't heard any other sign of a vehicle in the area, he eased back more. "We can get up, but I want you to take cover behind a car. Just in case."

He helped her to her feet as voices rang out from the entrance of the building. He stepped in front of Rachael to protect her.

"It was a gunshot!" a woman exclaimed. "Looks like that guy's been shot in the back."

"You were shot?" Rachael whipped around him so fast he couldn't stop her. She lightly ran a finger over the bullet hole. "Thankfully you wore a vest."

He moved behind her and eased her off to the side. "One of the first rules of law enforcement is that you have to take care of yourself first if you're going to help others, so I've learned to be prepared."

The minute the words left his mouth, he knew he was careful with his physical safety and well-being, but what about his mental health? Was he taking care there, or was he working so hard that he was burning himself out? And Rachael—was she doing the same thing?

They really were two of a kind. Maybe God had put them together so they could see their own behavior reflected in each other and realize how foolish it was. Maybe.

He tucked her behind a pillar, then turned his attention to the crowd. "Deputy Jake Marsh. I need you all to go back inside and remain there until I tell you it's safe."

Surprisingly, they complied, so when the police arrived to process the scene and take statements, it was handled in a systematic fashion. Even Skyler commented on how orderly things had been done before she fired questions at Rachael at the speed of a machine gun's bullets.

"Could you give us a minute to catch our breaths before you give us the third degree?" Jake asked, careful to insert humor in his tone to make it seem less demanding.

"There's nothing funny about this." Skyler pressed her finger on the bullet hole in Jake's jacket.

"Point taken," he answered, but stepped closer to Rachael. Not only because he wanted to be close to her, but because Skyler had the look of a leopard ready to pounce.

She fixed that penetrating gaze on Rachael. "Start from the moment you left the firehouse."

Rachael recounted the night in detail in a surprisingly calm voice, considering she was still shaken. He inserted a few comments to flesh out the story but let her tell her side, as she might have noticed things he hadn't picked up on.

"Did you get a good look at the shooter?" Skyler asked.

Rachael shook her head. "His head was down, so no."

"What about you, Jake? Did he look up when he fired?"

"Maybe, but by that time I was tackling Rachael to the ground, so I didn't catch his face."

"And it's clear you weren't looking at him when he shot you."

"Exactly," Jake replied. "I did get a good look at the car, though. It was a Honda Accord, and the first three digits of the plate match the stolen car I found in the database."

Skyler jotted the information on her notepad. "I think it's time to contact a TV station."

"The media?" Rachael asked. "Why?"

"Since the shooter was driving the stolen car we've already ID'd, we can assume this isn't some random homeless guy, and he's our kidnapper. The media will distribute the information, and ideally someone will see the car and call in."

"And what about the sketch?" Jake asked. "If Cash took care of that today, we can release that, as well."

"He got started on it, but unfortunately, the sketch artist was pulled to work on a murder. She'll meet with him again in the morning."

"So the minute they're finished, we'll show it to Rachael and then get it to the press," Jake said, hoping this information combined with the license plate would help them locate the car to process it for prints and provide the kidnapper's identity.

Skyler nodded. "I'll make sure you get the sketch."

"We also need to tell you about Lucy and Olin Kempner," Jake added, earning a disappointed look from Rachael.

But whether it disappointed Rachael or not, the couple seemed like a great lead—and Skyler had to track down any and every lead possible.

Later that night, Jake sat on the sofa, paperwork and his laptop lying next to him. He'd been trying to catch up on his work, but Rachael had joined him to walk the family room floor with a very fussy Kelly. Rachael said they thought the usually easygoing baby was experiencing a bout of colic, and she wouldn't quit crying. Rachael wanted Pam to get some sleep, so Rachael had checked in to see if he was awake. Once she found him doing paperwork, she brought the baby downstairs.

As Rachael paced the floor, he hadn't been able to take his eyes from her. She had no idea he was watching her. Her focus rested solely on the child, and every time she walked toward him, the longing in her eyes made his breath catch. She tenderly cradled the baby and softly cooed to her until she stopped wailing and hiccupped to a stop. Rachael's face beamed with happiness.

His thoughts went to the fund-raiser, and the way she'd displayed different sides of her personality. She'd been friendly with every person she met. Wealthy, impoverished, it didn't matter. She'd connected with them, but she'd also held herself in reserve. It wasn't until she'd discovered the snow, and her eyes had held the delight of a small child, that he'd experienced how carefree she could be.

The more he got to know her, the more he was coming to learn that she was a special woman. He was surprised she hadn't remarried yet and had a child of her own.

The thought of her with another man made his gut cramp, but he couldn't very well see himself in her life. Not with the way things were now.

She tiptoed across the room and settled Kelly into her swing. The rhythmic click of the swing lulled Jake into a sleepy mood, too, but it didn't seem to impact Rachael. She crossed to the Christmas tree and stared up at the top. He peered at the illuminated star casting yellow light onto the dark ceiling and wondered what she was thinking.

She turned and caught him watching her. Their eyes met for a moment, and anguish darkened her eyes.

Jake should mind his own business, and stay in his spot, but he couldn't leave her standing there alone. Not with her looking so forlorn.

He got up to join her. "I guess Kelly's asleep."

Rachael smiled. "For how long, I don't know, but I hope the swing will help her sleep."

"Then why are you so worried? Is it Kelly or everything else that's been going on?"

Her smile fell. "Who says I'm worried?"

He simply arched a brow.

"Okay, fine. I'm worried."

"We'll catch this guy, you know. He may be making it difficult, but we're good at our jobs, and *we will* find him. Then your life can go back to normal."

"I know, but..." She shrugged.

"But what, honey?" he said, before thinking about how intimate the word sounded.

"What if I don't want it to go back to normal? What if all I've been through the last few days has taught me that I want more from life?"

"Like children of your own?" he asked.

She took a step closer—why, he didn't know—but he liked her nearness and wouldn't argue over it.

The air around them was charged with heat as warm as the fireplace. The tree lights reflected sparkling shadows, leaving the room feeling as romantic as he could imagine, and he couldn't seem to pull his gaze from hers.

"You deserve to be a mother." He gently touched the side of her face.

"But I...I don't—"

"Shh." He pressed a finger to her lips. "Just accept that you're an amazing woman who would make an exceptional mother, and anything else that's been holding you back can disappear for the moment."

"Yes," she said breathlessly.

He took her yes to mean so much more, and he slid his fingers through her silky hair to the back of her neck and drew her even closer. He lowered his head, fully intending to kiss her, but paused first to be sure it was okay with her.

"Yes," she said again.

He pressed his lips against hers. Tentatively at first, but when she gave no resistance, he deepened the kiss. His head swam with how right kissing her felt, and before he lost control of his emotions, he lifted his head.

He wanted a wife and a family. That was certain now, but could he commit the time a wife and family would take? Could he let go of his guilt? Trust that God had put Rachael in his life for a reason beyond protecting her?

"I…" she said, pushing away, likely because of the uncertainty he was displaying. "We shouldn't."

Did she mean they shouldn't kiss? Shouldn't care for one another? In either case, they'd gone well beyond caring.

He opened his mouth to tell her so, but Kelly started whimpering from her swing. Rachael touched his cheek, her fingertips soft as a feather, then she walked over to Kelly, scooped her up and rushed from the room, as if running away from him.

He thought he'd been confused before, but he honestly couldn't have been any more perplexed than he felt now, and he didn't know how to move forward with her—or even if he should.

THIRTEEN

Over breakfast with Rachael, Jake stared at the text from Skyler.

Sid Cooper's a resident of the halfway house by vet's office. I can't talk to him until later today. If you're free, it would be great if you could question him.

So Sid Cooper, Pam's boyfriend with a rap sheet that included aggravated assault and armed robbery, lived close to the vet and close to where the car had been stolen.

Coincidence? Jake didn't think so.

He told Rachael about Sid. "I'll head over there straightaway, and I'd like you to stay here with Archer."

"Maybe I should come along to see if I recognize his voice."

"We all heard the intruder's voice on the center's video feed, so if he's our guy, I should be able to recognize him." Jake suspected that he might be wrong, and he wouldn't be sure of the man's voice, but after last night's attack, he didn't want to take Rachael out of the house. He also wouldn't expose her to such an unscrupulous guy unless absolutely necessary.

"I suppose you're right, and besides, I'm babysitting Kelly today. We wouldn't want to take her there."

"Exactly."

Jake arranged with Archer to cover Rachael's protection detail, then he drove to the halfway house and waited in the office while the manager went to get Sid.

He strode into the room, his shoulders back, a glare on a narrow face covered in acne scars. He wore torn jeans and a dingy T-shirt.

"I didn't do it," he said.

Jake resisted a smart-aleck comment about this being the common response from most criminals, and focused instead on the tenor of the man's voice. It was deep and gravelly, much like the kidnapper's, but then it could simply be the voice of a man who'd had a habit of inhaling drugs for years.

Jake gestured at a chair. "Why don't we sit down and talk."

Jake didn't wait for Sid to comply but took a seat on the edge of the desk, placing himself in a position to peer down on Sid.

Sid dropped into the chair, and his body seemed to sigh with the relief of not having to support itself. "What's this about?"

"Pam Baldwin. Do you remember her?"

"Pammy." He smiled, revealing rotting teeth, likely from a meth addiction. "Sure. We had some good times."

"Maybe these good times included fathering a child."

"Heard something about that." His tone didn't give Jake a hint of what the guy was thinking.

"Pam says you were together when she got pregnant."

"Yeah, man, yeah. I heard the kid was three months old. If that's true, we were together then."

"I know you and Pam aren't hanging in the same circles anymore, so exactly how are you keeping up with her?"

"A dude she works with lives here. We were talking about the good old days. He mentioned her."

It sounded like a logical explanation, but Jake wouldn't take it at face value, so he asked and received the name of Pam's coworker.

He jotted it in his notebook. "How does being a potential father make you feel?"

"Me, a dad?" He shook his head hard, sending greasy strands of hair sliding across his forehead. "Nah. I ain't got no interest in that. Not at all. I'm just busy keeping my own stuff together. Even if I wanted to—which, trust me, I don't—I can't take care of a kid."

"So you don't want anything to do with the baby, then?" Jake clarified.

"Nope. Nothing." He frowned. "Why're you asking me about the kid?"

"Where were you at 2:00 a.m. on Friday night?" Jake asked but didn't share why he wanted to know about Sid's whereabouts on the night of the vet's break-in.

He didn't answer for a moment, but his eyes narrowed. "That some kind of trick question? 'Cause bedtime check's at ten, and I'm always here for that."

"Okay, so that's where you were at ten. But where were you at two?"

"Here, man." He gnawed on the inside of his cheek. "Once we check in for the night, we aren't allowed to go out. If we do, we lose our place here. Can't risk that."

"What about Monday morning at six. Where were you then?" Jake didn't mention that this was the time of the attempted kidnapping.

"Here. My work shift starts at eight, so I was still here."

Jake scribbled the alibi information in the notebook and asked about the times for the pizza delivery and last night's shooting. Sid claimed he'd been at the halfway house both times.

"Is there anyone who can vouch for you for any of these times?"

"Maybe. Depends on how heavy the other guys were sleeping. Our beds are bunked in a room with six of us. You can ask them." He frowned again. "Say, what do you think I did, anyway?"

"I'm not at liberty to share that, but I appreciate your answers." Jake stood, ending the conversation. The guy's alibis were flimsy, and Jake didn't want Sid to know he was on his trail in case he tried to cover it up. "If I have additional questions, I'll get back to you."

Sid slunk out of the room, and Jake couldn't honestly say this guy's voice matched the man who'd tried to kidnap Kelly. If Sid's alibis didn't check out, Rachael would have to talk to him.

The manager stepped back into the office. He wore a frown and rubbed his hand over his shiny, bald scalp as if puzzled by something.

"Can I look at your bedtime checks for Sid?" Jake asked.

He shook his head. "I have to respect my residents' privacy rights."

"This is a matter of life and death." Jake made it sound as dire as he could.

"I suppose I could take a look at them and maybe answer your questions."

"Was Sid here on Friday night and last night at bed check?"

He waved a hand in the air. "That's an easy one. I'm sure he was here. If anyone is missing, the night supervisor is supposed to notify me of the missed check-in, as it's a condition of living here. Two strikes and the resident is out. If Sid was missing, it would have been his second strike, so the supervisor would have mentioned it."

"Can you check to be sure?" Jake asked.

"Sure." He retrieved a binder, then flipped a few pages and looked up, scratching his head. "Odd. No checkmark by Sid's name for Friday, and the night supervisor never reported it. Maybe he just made a mistake and didn't check the box."

"Can you confirm that with him?"

"Of course, but I don't want to wake him up, so it won't be until later this afternoon."

"That's fine." Jake flipped the page in his notebook. "I also need the names of Sid's roommates, and I need to talk to each of them."

"Sorry," he said, snapping the binder closed, "but I can't give out the names. Privacy again."

"Can you arrange for me to talk to them?"

"Most of them are still having breakfast, so I'll ask if they want to speak to you, and if they do, I'll send them in one at a time."

"Perfect," Jake replied, thankful the manager was being as cooperative as he could while still observing his privacy rules.

Jake settled into a chair and for the next hour interviewed five men, all wearing the ravages of habitual drug use on their faces. Not one of them could vouch for Sid the morning of the attempted kidnapping or for the other incidents. It didn't mean Sid was guilty of attempted kidnapping, but he went to the top of Jake's suspect list.

When he got back to the firehouse, he'd arrange for Rachael to meet with Sid after work to see if his voice jogged her memory, but first Jake wanted to stop by the

Portland Police Bureau's Central Precinct to take a look at the evidence from the veterinary office break-in.

Detective Lewis was cordial enough, but he watched Jake with a careful eye as he sifted through the box of items collected at the break-in. Jake found typical items bagged and tagged by the forensic staff—glass shards, fingerprints, a scrap of fabric—but one item, a piece of hard, glassy plastic, caught Jake's attention. He pulled out the evidence bag and studied it.

Golden in color, the object was an inch long and half an inch wide and thick. One side was rounded and the other jagged, as if the plastic had broken off a larger item. He checked the evidence tag to learn the criminalist found it by the window Jake had seen the thief enter on the video.

"Ever discover what this is for?" Jake asked the detective.

Lewis shook his head. "It would take a hard impact to cause the break in such solid plastic so it might not have belonged to the burglar."

"He could have had the object in his pocket, and when he landed on the windowsill, it snapped and fell out."

"Could be," Lewis said, but he clearly didn't believe it.

"Mind if I take a picture of it?"

"Sure, go ahead."

Jake dug out his camera and snapped a few shots from different angles. He filed thoughts of the item in the back of his mind in case something came up later, and then he moved on. He searched through the other items and stopped at a torn piece of clothing that could have been ripped from a black hoodie like the one the suspect had worn when he tried to take Kelly.

"Recovered that on a nail by the window," Lewis said before Jake could ask. "Likely the burglar's jacket."

"Any hope that you found a manufacturer who uses this fabric?"

Lewis snorted. "For a burglary? Nah, we don't have that kind of time."

"I'd like to have it analyzed," Jake said. "What about the hair fibers? Any DNA analysis done?"

"Time and money, man," Lewis said. "In a low-profile case like this, we don't process DNA until we have a suspect to compare it to. Never found a suspect."

"I'd like to get the DNA run, too, so we can compare it to the DNA recovered from our kidnapping attempt."

"Sure. Knock yourself out. You're welcome to fill out the mounds of paperwork it'll take for our agencies to coordinate on this task."

"Oh, don't worry," Jake said with confidence. "I'm good at cutting through the bureaucracy, and we'll be sending these off to the lab before I leave your building. You can count on that."

The day had passed without incident, and as Rachael lifted Kelly to her shoulder, she felt a sense of relief that nothing bad had happened. Jake sat in a recliner, arranging an appointment for her to speak with Sid Cooper. Jake had already told her that he was able to send off hair and fabric for analysis from the break-in, and he was also hoping to get a sample of saliva from Sid for a DNA comparison, too.

Cash stepped into the room. "The sketch artist is finally free, and I'm off to meet with her. I'll call Skyler as soon as we have a solid sketch."

"Can you make sure it's sent to Logan as soon as possible, too?"

"Logan, as in Detective Hunter's husband?" Rachael asked. "Why him?"

"The FBI has state-of-the-art facial recognition software," Jake explained. "As an agent, Logan can run the sketch through it."

"And if all goes well, we'll know the suspect's ID before the day is out." Cash spun and headed for the front door.

Jake returned his focus to his phone and dialed. Rachael realized Kelly had fallen asleep, so she stood to take Kelly to her portable crib upstairs.

"Hold up, Rachael," Detective Hunter called out from the office doorway.

Rachael turned, and when she saw the tight look on the detective's face, Rachael tried not to cringe. She'd come to recognize Detective Hunter's expressions, and Rachael knew she wasn't going to like what was coming next. As the detective stepped into the room, Rachael nuzzled Kelly's soft curls to keep her mind positive.

Detective Hunter stopped near Rachael, her feet planted wide as if ready to do battle. "I need to talk to you and Jake once he's off the phone."

Rachael glanced at Jake, and he held up a finger. Surprisingly, the detective turned her attention to Kelly. Her expression softened, and her eyes held tender affection, a look Rachael hadn't seen from this tough detective before.

"Would you like to hold her?" Rachael asked.

"Me?" Detective Hunter shook her head. "I don't know the first thing about babies."

"Maybe it's time you learned." Rachael put Kelly into the detective's arms while giving her instructions on how to hold her.

She cocooned Kelly like a fragile butterfly, and when Kelly made a mewling noise, the detective started bouncing her.

"You might not want to do that," Rachael warned. "She's just finished her bottle, and she might spit up."

"Oh, yeah, right. Okay. Anything else I need to know?" She sounded unsure, an emotion foreign to her take-charge attitude.

At the thought of a tiny baby unsettling this woman, Rachael almost chuckled, but she managed to hold it back. "She's a pretty easygoing baby except for this recent colic. Some babies suffer with it for months, and they cry nonstop."

The detective's head popped up, fear rampant in her gaze. "What happens if you have a baby who's not so easygoing?"

"You deal with it and find lots of support." Rachael eyed the detective and thought about how she'd been so sick lately. Perhaps these questions and the fear meant she was pregnant and terrified of being a mother.

Rachael couldn't allow the poor woman's fear to linger. "For example, if you were to have a baby, you have all of your friends on the FRS and their significant others. That's a large number of people who can give you a break."

"Yeah, you're right." She smiled and seemed to relax a bit. "I have great support."

"Yes, you do."

Jake pocketed his phone and stood to join them. "You needed to talk to us."

And just like that, a curtain came down over Detective Hunter's fear and anxiety, and she handed Kelly back to Rachael.

"I just finished viewing the traffic cams near the Baldwins' house. Pam's father left home Monday morning despite claiming he stayed home."

"So he could be involved, then," Jake said.

Detective Hunter nodded. "I'll contact his lawyer and get him into the office to question him again. Also, you should know the DNA from the hair found on Rachael's clothes didn't return a match in the database."

"Which means what, exactly?" Rachael asked.

"Means that if the hair is from any of our suspects—Sid, Hal, Pam's father, your friends in CAR—they haven't had a DNA sample taken by a law enforcement agency."

"So it really doesn't tell you anything," Rachael said.

"It tells me that in order to move forward, I'll need to secure DNA samples from our list of suspects. Not you, of course, as we already know it's not your hair. Though…" She paused and locked gazes with Rachael. "I have to say, after what I just discovered, your name will remain on my suspect list."

"Me?" Rachael's heart creased at the seriousness of her tone. "What do you mean?"

"Why didn't you tell us about your miscarriage? Was it to keep us from thinking that you might want to replace your baby with Kelly?"

"Miscarriage?" Jake asked, his face contorting in stunned disbelief.

Rachael watched him, his pain clear and unsettling. She wanted to take him aside to explain that Detective Hunter was all wrong; Rachael would never consider replacing her loss by abducting Kelly. She could never cause another mother to go through the same pain she'd experienced. Instead, she'd taken the positive approach to assuaging her guilt by helping parents who were at risk of losing their children.

"Care to explain?" Detective Hunter asked.

Rachael didn't want to tell the detective anything, but she did want Jake to know what had happened, so she kept her focus on him. His initial shock subsided and he seemed willing to remain in the room to hear her explanation.

"After Eli died," she said, "I was in such a state of grief, I couldn't eat or sleep. My health suffered, and a month after he died, I miscarried. I was at the beginning of my fifth month."

Tears pricked at Rachael's eyes, but she fought them back and kept her gaze on Jake. "I'm to blame for losing my child. If I'd taken better care of myself, she might be alive today." She took a step closer to Jake. "You understand how I feel, right? You thought you could have saved your family."

He nodded, and again she was thankful that he was at least communicating with her.

"You really think it's your fault?" the detective asked.

"The doctor said I wasn't to blame, but my heart says otherwise."

"Why didn't you tell me?" Jake clamped his hand on the back of his neck, a sure sign that he was stressed.

"First, I've felt so guilty about not taking care of myself that I've never told anyone about it. Not even when my good friend Annie tried to help me cope."

"And second?" he asked.

"You told me the other day that losing a baby fit an abductor's profile, and I already fit all of the other criteria, so I knew it would make me a prime suspect."

Detective Hunter started to speak, but Rachael held up her hand.

"I don't care if you investigate me. I have nothing to hide. I'm innocent, but I thought if you spent your time on me, the real kidnapper would get away."

"You should have given us more credit to discern the facts," Jake said. "At least me, anyway."

"I know, Jake, and I'm sorry. I should have told you. Can you forgive me?"

He nodded, but she could see the lingering hurt in his eyes and her own visceral response to hurting him cut her to the core.

If she'd wondered if more than attraction flowed between them, she now knew there was more—much more—on both of their sides.

Jake had to get out of the house. To get away. To think. Fortunately it was almost time to pick Pam up from work, so he took off. He arrived at the grocery store early and sat in the parking lot to wait for her shift to end. He tapped a thumb on the steering wheel—his way of pacing and working through the miscarriage bombshell.

He didn't for one minute believe the miscarriage meant Rachael was involved in trying to abduct Kelly, but he did believe she'd purposely misled him. And he didn't even blame her for that. Not really. Guilt kept mouths shut. He knew that. He didn't go around telling people about his role the day his family died, but he had told her, because he cared about her.

There, he admitted it. He cared about her. A lot. And he thought she reciprocated the feelings and they were based on mutual respect and sharing. But maybe he was wrong. He wouldn't know until he had a chance to process the news, and then sit down and talk to her about it.

Pam opened the door of his truck, bringing him back to the present.

"You were a long way off," she said as she climbed in.

"I've got a lot on my mind." He cranked the engine and shifted into Drive.

Pam clicked on her seat belt. "Would it be okay if we

stopped by my apartment to pick up a few things for Kelly?"

"No problem." Jake appreciated more time away from Rachael to think, as discussing the miscarriage with her was too important to botch.

"Anything new in the investigation?" Pam asked.

He shared the leads they'd uncovered that day. "Skyler is trying to get your dad's lawyer to arrange a meeting with him, but so far she's struck out."

"Not surprising." Pam shook her head in slow, sorrowful arcs. "I totally burned my bridges with them. They tried to help me so many times, and I stomped all over them. That's not uncommon for addicts. Not that I'm making an excuse, because I treated them badly and don't deserve another chance."

"You've gotten your life back on track," Jake said. "And you deserve another chance."

"Honestly, I wish that was true, but I wonder if I'd take it if they offered it."

"I don't follow."

"I live life one day at a time. I still wake up with cravings every morning. And when life throws me a curveball, I consider scoring some meth, and I'm afraid I'll wind up hurting my parents again after I've already caused them so much grief."

He felt her pain, knew her guilt and hated to see it keep her from the best life had to offer.

"You have to let go of your past and move on," he said, shocked at the words coming out of his mouth. He didn't practice what he preached, nor did Rachael, and it had put secrets between them and was keeping them apart.

Pam sighed. "Easy to say. Not so easy to do."

"True, I know, but you've got a lot of people on your side supporting you and helping make sure you don't slip. Let them support you so you won't fail. Then, if we find out your parents aren't involved in the kidnapping attempt, go talk to them when this is all over."

"Maybe," she said and fell silent.

Jake knew the word *maybe*. Knew it well. Had lived it for years whenever he wondered if there was life beyond the guilt he felt over his family's death.

Well, no more. He would take his own advice starting right now, and he wouldn't go with the maybes in his life anymore. He lifted his guilt to God in a silent prayer, and for the first time, left it with God.

Jake would live each day new, as he'd told Pam to do. Take things as they came and stop thinking God should change his situation, but instead, live in the situation God placed him in.

Like now. He'd talk to Rachael as soon as he could. Tell her that he cared about her and ask if she wanted to start dating after they jailed the intruder. Then if she said yes, Jake would let God take charge and deal with any lingering fears.

Excited about the possibilities for their future, he turned onto the street for Pam's apartment. She dug out her keys from her backpack. Her bright gold key chain grabbed Jake's attention.

He pointed the truck into a parking space and turned to her. "Can I see your key chain?"

She shrugged and handed it to him. He ran his finger over the hard plastic and then dug out his phone to look at the plastic piece recovered from the vet's office. They were a match.

"Where'd you get this?" he asked.

"My key chain?"

He nodded.

"It's from CAR's drug recovery program. The gold

color signifies six months sober, and people in the program receive the key chain in an awards ceremony."

"So there are a bunch of people with the same one?"

"Yes. Their six-month success rate is very high."

Thoughts and questions whirled through Jake's mind. "How long have they been giving them out?"

"I think they started handing them out about the time I got mine, but if it's important to know the exact date, you could ask William or Ursula. They'd know."

Important? he thought. It could very well be the breakthrough they sought in the kidnapping investigation.

FOURTEEN

Rachael laid Kelly in her portable crib in Jake's condo and patted her back until she drifted off to sleep. Usually caring for Kelly made Rachael happy, but even the precious child didn't lift her spirits after Jake's reaction to Skyler's bombshell. Rachael wanted to talk with him privately, but he'd raced right out to pick up Pam from work.

On the bright side, he'd taken the news far better than she'd expected, and she knew they could work things out if they just had some time alone.

She turned on the baby monitor and stepped into the hall. She heard the front door open and rushed down the hallway. But Pam stepped inside alone and Rachael's feet faltered on the landing before she jogged down the stairs. "I just put Kelly down for a nap."

Pam yawned. "Then I'm going to take a quick nap, too."

"Before you go up, can you tell me where Jake is?"

"He said I should tell you that he has an errand to run and that Detective Hunter will stay here with you." Pam trudged up the steps.

Rachael found herself with nothing to do but dwell on her issue with Jake, and that wasn't healthy. She needed to focus on something else. Someone else.

Gloria. Rachael had promised to call and check up on her friend today, and now was the perfect time. She strode into the living room and settled on the sofa to dial.

"'Lo," Gloria answered.

"It's Rachael," she replied. "William told me you weren't feeling well, and I wanted to check on you."

"Nothing's 'smatter with me. I'm fine."

Fine. Hardly. She was slurring her words and sounded out of it.

"Gloria," Rachael said. "Is William home with you?"

"'Sworking. Bye."

"Gloria. Don't go. Gloria, are you there?" Rachael asked, but her phone displayed a disconnected call. Gloria had hung up on her.

Rachael quickly redialed, but the phone rang and rang until the voice mail picked up.

"Gloria, please call me back," Rachael said after the beep. "I'm worried about you."

She hung up and dialed William but got his voice mail. She left an urgent message asking him to call her back as soon as possible.

She couldn't sit by and do nothing, so she got up and paced the floor, anxiously waiting for a return call. Thirty minutes passed, but she didn't hear from William or Gloria. She called him again. Got his voice mail again. Left a more urgent message. Tried Gloria. Same thing.

"That settles it," she mumbled, and headed for the office to talk to Detective Hunter.

Sitting behind her computer, she looked up, her gaze a mix of questions and surprise.

"I know I'm not on your list of favorite people right now, but I need a favor," Rachael said bluntly.

"What do you need?"

She quickly told her about Gloria. "I'd call 911, but

William is very protective of their privacy, and he would be mortified if their name made the news for no reason."

"So you want me to take you over there to check on her?"

"Yes, please. Would you?"

She seemed to war with the decision, and finally shrugged. "It's safe enough, I suppose. There's no way anyone would know where we were going, and I can make sure we're not followed."

"Thank you." Rachael stepped out the door before the detective changed her mind.

At the front door, Detective Hunter shrugged into her coat. "I commend you on your passion and concern for helping your friend."

"Friend. Oh, no, Pam. We can't leave her and Kelly alone here."

"Brady's out back tinkering with his truck. I'll get him to stand duty."

"And I'll run up and tell Pam." Rachael charged up the stairs and returned to the front door with her coat and purse in a few minutes.

Detective Hunter met her in the entryway. "Same rules apply as when you leave the house with Jake. Stay close. Don't dawdle, and listen to my every command. Got it?"

Even with her intense questioning, Rachael had not seen this side of the detective, and the authority she carried impressed Rachael. "Got it."

They hurried to her vehicle, a white SUV with a sheriff decal on the side.

"One of the perks of being an investigator," she said, unlocking the door.

They both hopped in, and even with the circuitous route the detective took to make sure they weren't being followed, they arrived at Gloria's house in fifteen minutes.

"Wow." The detective peered up at the two-story house in the West Hills of Portland, a very affluent area of town.

"They may be quite wealthy, but they're just regular people like you and me. And they have hearts the size of this house."

She swiveled to look at Rachael. "Are you saying I don't have a big heart?"

"No...what—"

"Just kidding with you, Rachael."

"Oh, that's you kidding. I've never seen it." *Or heard you call me Rachael.*

"Ouch." Detective Hunter mocked pulling a knife from her chest. "But I deserve it after the way I pushed you so hard. It was just a strategy. I had to keep after you to see if you'd break. Nothing personal, you understand."

"Nothing personal? It was very personal to me, Detective. Especially when you brought up the miscarriage. You should know I would never—never!—put another mother through the pain of loss that I experienced."

"I believe you," she said, sounding sincere. "I've pretty much believed you from day one."

"But you...you've declared my guilt all along."

"I was just doing my job, which means whether I believe you or not, I have to keep investigating you until I find proof to back up your statements."

Rachael knew she was right, but it had still been painful, and all she could do was stare at the detective.

"Look," she said. "You wanted a detective who was good at her job to work this case, didn't you? Well, I'm good at my job, and I'm very thorough."

Rachael nodded, but didn't think it would be easy to forget the pain that the detective had caused. "Let's check on Gloria."

Outside, the detective hustled to the front door, and

Rachael kept up. She rang the doorbell and also knocked on the door. As time ticked by and Gloria didn't answer, Rachael pounded harder and pressed the bell several times.

Finally she heard footsteps crossing the foyer, and the door opened.

"Rach!" Gloria exclaimed. Her eyes were unfocused, and she still wore silk pajamas and slippers. Her hair was a ratty mess, and circles of mascara hung under her eyes.

"You sounded odd on the phone, so I came to check on you," Rachael said.

Gloria stepped back and made a big sweeping gesture with her arm. She lost her balance, and Rachael grabbed her friend's elbow before she fell. That's when Rachael smelled alcohol on her breath.

She guided Gloria through the door and to the sofa. Rachael saw no sign of alcohol in the room, but Gloria acted inebriated. Detective Hunter mimicked taking a drink out of a bottle, and Rachael nodded her agreement.

"Have you been celebrating?" Rachael asked.

"C'brating." Gloria shook her head hard and fell over on the sofa. She righted herself. "Lass thing I'd be doing."

"Has William called you?"

"No. He's too busy saving people," she said scornfully.

"I thought you liked working with CAR, too."

"I do. Juss don't like the work he's been doing." A derisive scowl followed her words.

"Seems like you might benefit from a nap," Detective Hunter suggested.

Gloria scratched her head. "I am sleepy."

"Why don't we help you up to your bed?" Rachael offered and brought Gloria to her feet.

She wobbled, and the detective took the other side to

steady Gloria. They started for the stairs, but the color drained from Detective Hunter's face.

"Not you, too," Rachael mumbled.

"Can you handle this?" She clamped a hand over her mouth. "I'm gonna be sick."

"Bathroom's just down the hall." Rachael pointed at the first-floor bathroom she'd used many times when visiting Gloria.

The detective ran for the bathroom, and Rachael managed to get Gloria into her bed. She was softly snoring within moments. Rachael stood watching her friend. As a refined and mannerly woman, she would never get sloppy drunk like this unless something terrible had upset her. She'd commented about William's work, so maybe her binge was related to that. And it could also be the reason he didn't answer his phone or call her back.

Well, Rachael wasn't leaving Gloria alone until she got some answers. She'd keep calling William until he either picked up or stepped through that door, whichever came first.

Jake approached the young woman with spiked purple hair sitting behind CAR's reception desk.

"Is William Franks in?" he asked.

She shook her head, looking bored to death.

"How about Ursula?"

"Nah, they're both meeting with potential donors." She looked at her green nails as if they held more interest than he did.

With William and Ursula both out of the office, this girl was the only one who could give Jake the information he needed. He feared she'd cite privacy rules and balk at his request.

He was in no mood to be turned down, so he pulled

out his badge and gave her a no-nonsense look. "I need a list of anyone who has received your gold key chains this past year."

"I—"

He held up his hand. "Before you tell me you can't give me a list, let me tell you a baby's life is on the line if you don't comply."

"A baby?"

"Only three months old," Jake added, not feeling the least bit guilty playing on her sympathies.

Her eyes creased, and she nodded before turning to the computer screen.

It seemed as if she really didn't care much about her job, or maybe he'd actually scared her. Either way, the printer next to the monitor soon spit out a page, and she handed it to him.

He ran his gaze down the paper. The name Thad Wofford caught his attention. William had mentioned that his assistant, Thad, was enrolled in their sobriety program. Maybe he could tell Jake about the others on the list.

He looked at the receptionist. "Thad Wofford. He's William's assistant, right?"

She nodded.

"Can you point me to his office?"

"Third door on the right—"

"Thanks, I got it," he said and took off before she could stop him.

He stepped into the small office boasting little personality except for a picture perched on the credenza of a man receiving the key chain from William. Jake assumed Thad was the recipient, but he wasn't in his office. Perhaps the receptionist had been about to tell him that Thad had gone to the meeting, too.

Jake turned to leave, and the phone rang. An answering machine picked up on the third ring. "You have reached the office of William Franks. I'm unable to take your call right now, so please leave a detailed message, and I'll get back to you as soon as I can."

The machine beeped, and a woman's voice came over the speaker.

"Thad, my name's Rachael Long."

Rachael?

"I'm friends with Gloria and William. Gloria isn't feeling well, and I've been trying to get ahold of William, but he's not answering his cell or calling me back. So I thought I'd try this line, too, in case William's phone is dead. If he's there, please have him come straight home. I'll stay at his house until he arrives." She rattled off her phone number as Jake tried to come to grips with the fact that Rachael was at William's house and not at the firehouse.

He dialed Skyler. The phone rang five times, and she didn't answer. He called Rachael next. She didn't answer, either.

"They could be taking care of Gloria and can't answer right now," he mumbled to calm his concern.

Or maybe Rachael didn't want to talk to him after he'd left without talking with her about the miscarriage. He didn't blame her, and knew it would have bothered him if the situation was reversed.

He called the firehouse to see if anyone could tell him what was going on.

"Brady Owens," Brady answered.

"Rachael and Skyler. Where are they?"

"They went over to check on some woman named Gloria."

Jake's anxiety grew. "Neither one of them is answering the phone, and I want to check on them. Look up

William or Gloria Frank's address in the DMV database and text it to me."

"Roger that," Brady replied, and they disconnected.

Jake tapped his foot until his phone chimed with the text. Jake thanked him, then entered the address into his GPS.

The answering machine beeped again, and he heard it play Rachael's message, then the glowing red light that signaled a pending message went dark. Jake hadn't worked an answering machine in years, but he believed that Thad or William had just remotely accessed the machine, listened to the message and deleted it.

Jake exited the building and jumped into his car, then set out for the West Hills. He'd just made it through Portland's heavy traffic when his phone chimed, indicating another text. At the stoplight, he glanced at the device mounted on his dash.

The text was from Cash. He'd attached a scanned copy of his sketch of the delivery driver. Jake thumbed to the picture, and his heart plummeted.

Looking beyond the disguise, he could see the man's eyes, nose and cheekbones. Jake had just seen that exact face on a picture in Thad's office.

Thad Wofford was the kidnapper.

But why? What was his motive? Could he be Kelly's father?

Didn't matter now, did it?

Thad was the man who'd been trying to kill Rachael, and if he was the one who'd just accessed William's messages, she'd given him her exact location.

FIFTEEN

Rachael stepped into the hallway to keep from waking Gloria and dialed William again. Her phone signaled another incoming call, but she ignored it. William didn't answer, so Rachael left another message, then looked at the missed call on her phone.

Jake. His second call. Something important must be happening. She didn't bother listening to his message, but dialed him right back.

"Rachael. Good. Good. You're all right." His words tumbled out and the tone of his voice verged on panic.

She'd never heard him sound so unsettled.

"Why wouldn't I be okay?" she asked.

"William's assistant, Thad. He's the kidnapper."

"What?" She laughed. "That's crazy."

"I know it sounds crazy, but I just left his office. His picture is on the desk. I compared it to the sketch Cash had made. He might have been wearing a disguise as the driver, but it's clearly him."

"Are you sure, or do you just want it to be him?"

"I'm sure."

She still couldn't believe it. Maybe Jake had mixed something up.

"I'm on my way over there," he continued, "but I need you to be careful until I arrive."

She heard the front door open. "I think William's home."

"Good. If it is indeed William and not Thad," he said. "Where's Skyler?"

"In the bathroom downstairs, throwing up. I think she's pregnant."

"I think you're right," Jake said. "Can you see the door? Is it William?"

She still didn't believe Thad was a kidnapper, but she crept toward the stairs in case she really was in danger. A young man talking on his phone stepped inside. His voice was low and secretive like he didn't want to be overheard, but Rachael could hear him just fine.

"This ends today," he said. "I'm going to clean up this problem with Rachael once and for all." He paused as if listening.

"I don't care what you want, William." He faced out the front window. "I'm the one who'll take the heat for attempted kidnapping and murder. Not you."

William? William's involved?

Rachael gasped.

No. No. Thad had to have heard her.

He spun. Looked up. Their gazes connected.

The face. The voice. It all came flooding back to her. Him standing over her. The gun in his hand. His warnings. The syringe. Ripping off his mask.

"You're right," she whispered into the phone as she backed away. "It's him. Thad's the kidnapper, and he just saw me."

"Hide," Jake warned. "Or get to Skyler, whichever you can do without him seeing you."

"He's on his way over to the stairway, and I'd have

to pass him to get to Detective Hunter." Rachael back-pedaled across the carpet, but her every step seemed to be in slow motion, and she wasn't moving fast enough.

She heard Thad take the first step, a loud thud that echoed through the space. She let out a breath and waited for her thumping heart to slow.

"Are you in a safe place?" Jake asked.

"Not yet."

"Move quickly. Now!"

She spun and ran toward the master bedroom.

"I'm on my way," Jake said. "Just a few miles out."

A quick glance back told her Thad had tracked her movements and was coming for her. "Please hurry, Jake. He's going to kill me."

"Don't panic. I'm almost there, and so is my team," Jake said to Rachael as calmly as he could. He was thankful he'd thought to call in the FRS the moment he'd learned about Thad. "And most important of all, don't hang up."

"I'm in Gloria's bedroom," she whispered. "She's sleeping in the bed. Should I hide under it or in the closet?"

"He'll go to the closet first. So hide on the far side of the bed, and when he steps into the closet, run from the room and get outside."

"But he has a gun."

"I know, honey, but even if you hide under the bed, he'll still have the gun, and he will for sure see you there."

"Okay... Oh, Jake... I'm sorry. I should have told you about the miscarriage, I—"

"Shh, don't think about that now. Everything is fine between us."

"But I wanted you to know that I'm sorry. In case he… you know…finds me."

"He won't. Just stay calm." Jake couldn't believe he could tell her to stay calm when his own heart was racing.

He prayed like he hadn't prayed in years, imploring God to keep Rachael safe and allow him to arrive on time.

"I'm behind the bed." Her voice, only a whisper, came through his phone. "He's just outside the room."

"Put the phone in your pocket so you're ready to run. I'll still be able to hear what's going on."

"Okay. Here goes."

He heard the static ruffling as she shoved her cell into her pocket. A vision of her in that room with a killer a few feet away flooded Jake's brain and nearly had him running into the ditch. He jerked the car back onto the road.

He hadn't called the local police, as he feared they would botch things and cause a hostage standoff that could result in the loss of her life, but he would be on the scene in a few moments and could direct the action, so he grabbed his radio and called in backup from the PPB. He made sure dispatch relayed the fact that he was in charge and everyone should stand down until he ordered them to help.

Then he floored the gas and prayed he'd made the right decision.

Rachael held her breath and waited, her senses on hyperalert. The soft carpet fibers under her fingers felt rough and irritating. The smell of Gloria's cloying perfume was nauseating.

Footsteps whispered across the floor. She heard Gloria's closet door whip open. The space almost the size of a room and L-shaped, Thad would have to go all the way inside to check for her.

She risked a quick peek over the bed. The room was empty. She jumped to her feet. Her legs shook, and they barely held her. She ran for the stairs. Raced down them and jerked open the door.

"I'm outside," she told Jake, hoping he heard her voice with the phone in her pocket. "Hurry."

Without a jacket, the cold sucked away her body heat, but she ignored it and ran as hard as she could down the winding driveway toward the hilly road. She nearly lost her footing a few times, but she soon neared the road.

A sharp crack split the air, and the concrete at Rachael's feet exploded. Shards ricocheted up, pelting her body and piercing her cheek.

Another crack. Something whizzed past her arm, ripping into the flesh on the way. It was a bullet. She'd been shot.

She screamed and dove behind a stand of azaleas. She scooted to her knees and peered out through the shrubbery. Thad came rushing down the hill, a weapon in his hand, his gaze searching the area. He paused and turned. She had to move before he caught her.

Fearing a bullet in her back, she ran hard. Down the hill. Toward the gate. Blood poured down her arm and dripped, leaving a trail. She reached for the button to open the gate, but the gate suddenly swung open and a big silver sedan entered the driveway.

William.

She slipped into nearby bushes and peeked around them in time to see Thad duck into tall conifers lining the driveway. Odd. Why was he hiding from William?

The car inched closer, now ten feet away.

She waited for the large sedan to come even with her, and then she squeezed behind the tall brick pillar holding the wrought iron gate.

William stopped. The car door groaned open.

She pulled her phone from her pocket and whispered, "Don't talk or they'll hear you. I'm at the gate. Thad shot me, and William just arrived."

"Thad?" William called out. "Show yourself." William took a few steps, inching closer to her, crunching over gravel.

She saw the face she'd trusted for years. The man she'd been friends with for so long. But after hearing Thad's call with William, she knew she couldn't trust him. Wishing she could hear Jake's comforting voice or see his truck pull into the drive, Rachael got ready to run again.

Her heart raced, thumping in her chest as if it wanted to escape, the ringing in her ears threatening to take her down.

"This isn't funny, Thad. Where are you?" William called again.

The barrel of Thad's gun poked through the branches. He probably thought she was distracted by William, and he could use that chance to kill her.

No. She'd use it to make her escape.

She had to go. Had to run. Run hard. Now! And hope she could outrun a speeding bullet.

"If you don't show yourself, Rachael," Thad shouted, "I will kill William."

Rachael didn't think she should trust Thad, but could she take a chance that he would shoot William? He was involved in this somehow, but that didn't mean she wanted him to die.

"I mean it, Rachael," Thad said convincingly. "I'll kill him."

Rachael wished she could run, but she had to help William. She searched the area and couldn't come up with a way to protect him besides surrendering to Thad.

Think, think, think.

All she had was the heavy snow piling up at her feet.

Snow—that was it! She could pelt Thad with snowballs so William could run, too.

She shoved her phone back into her pocket and dropped to her knees. The snow was wet and perfect for making tight, heavy balls. The icy cold bit into her fingers, but she kept packing them tight, and she quickly formed a stack.

"Last chance, Rachael!" Thad called.

Rachael peeked out and calculated the distance. She could do this.

She grabbed the first ball and hurled it. The snow smacked Thad in the face, and she was thankful for all of her years playing softball in high school. He flailed to brush it off, letting his gun hand drop.

"Run, William!" she yelled and fired off another ball, then another and another.

She heard William's feet pounding down the driveway, but she kept tossing the snowballs until he got even with her.

"Hurry, William," she said. "Join me behind the brick."

He stepped around the column. She fired off a few more snowballs, her teeth starting to chatter and the cold sinking into her limbs.

"Now what?" William asked.

"Now we run." She turned and handed him a few snowballs. "C'mon. We have to keep throwing these as we run, so when Thad gets off a shot, his aim is off."

She didn't wait for him to agree, but charged onto the driveway, pelting a snowball at Thad as she did. He guarded his face, and she hurled another one, then bolted through the open gate. She heard William behind her, but she couldn't turn to look or she might lose her footing on the slippery drive.

She reached the narrow road, turned toward the main highway and picked up speed. She glanced back and saw William behind her. They'd gone half a mile when Thad called out from the road, "Stop or I'll shoot!"

"The woods," she said to William. "It's our only chance."

She swerved to the side and plunged into a ditch, her feet getting tangled in the deep snow, nearly taking her down.

Calm down. You can do this.

She righted herself and climbed up the incline to the protective cover of the wooded area. William was right behind her.

She ran as hard and fast as she could while lifting her feet above the foot of snow. She hit a clearing and spotted a lake ahead, cutting off her path. It was large, and the underbrush prevented her from going around it. Her only option was to cross over.

She started forward.

"No!" William called out. "Look at the sign. It's not safe."

She'd seen the Caution: Thin Ice sign, but she had no other choice. She continued forward and reached the edge of the lake.

She put her foot on the ice and tested it. It held. She took another step. The ice remained solid, and she moved forward until she was well on her way. She glanced back at William standing in the middle of the clearing.

"It's fine, William!" she shouted. "C'mon."

"For you, maybe, but I weigh a lot more than you."

She couldn't force him to join her, but she didn't want to leave him behind, either.

Father, please tell me what to do.

Thad suddenly bounded into the clearing.

"Hands up, William," he commanded as he advanced.

Rachael quickly estimated the distance between her and Thad. She was within his range, but William was much closer.

"Don't move, Rachael!" Thad yelled as he placed the gun against William's temple.

"I'm sorry, Rachael," William said. "I didn't mean for this to happen."

"Shut up." Thad pushed William forward.

With Thad's focus on William as he marched him toward the water, Rachael's attention went to trying to rescue herself. She remembered the phone in her pocket. She slipped it out and held it in her palm so Jake could better hear the conversation.

"I should never have stepped onto the lake!" Rachael yelled at Thad, not to warn him, but to make sure Jake knew where she had gone. "The ice isn't safe."

"Exactly." Thad laughed. "Once William joins you out there, it's sure to crack, and you'll both sink into a watery grave."

"Don't do this, Thad," William begged.

"You wanted me to do this." Thad shoved William forward. "Remember? Coming to me. Begging. Saying you'd give me a million bucks to kidnap your kid, and I could finally get out from under my debt."

Rachael shot a look at William. "Kelly's your child?"

He nodded. "I had an affair with Pam. She was a friend of one of our clients and so hopped up on drugs that if she told anyone they'd never believe her."

"How long have you known Kelly was yours?"

"Not long." He ran a hand over his face, and she thought he might cry. "We've never told anyone, but Gloria hasn't been able to get pregnant. When Pam did, I decided to do a DNA test on Kelly just in case I was the father. I couldn't believe it when the results proved she was my child. She was the answer to my prayers, and I had to find a way to have her in my life." He spun on Thad. "But I never authorized you to terrorize or try to kill Rachael. I only wanted Kelly in my life without all the scandal that would hit the media when the truth of my affair got out."

"An affair with a woman who was strung out on drugs when you claimed to help women just like her," Thad added.

"I'd be ruined."

"Especially if they found out you'd also been with many other women in the program," Thad sneered. "If this hit the media, those women would come forward."

William clamped his hands over his ears. "Stop. Don't say any more. I can't help it. I tried to stop."

"What about Gloria?" Rachael asked. "Does she know about this?"

"About the women, but not Kelly. I couldn't tell her that. We've been in the process of adopting a child, but since I have Kelly, why would I adopt another one? I don't want another man's child."

"She's not just your child. She's Pam's, too. Did you consider that?" Rachael asked.

William frowned. "Pam would suffer at first, but you see how hard she's struggling just to give Kelly the bare necessities. Gloria and I could give her so much more and do a much better job of raising her." He took a deep breath. "Don't look at me like that. You know the recidivism rates for drug addicts. With all the obstacles facing Pam, she wouldn't remain sober long. Then what? Kelly would be taken away from Pam anyway, and might even go into foster care. Why let that happen when Gloria and I have everything to give to Kelly?"

"And how did you plan to suddenly show up with a baby?"

"Adoption."

"But Pam would know it was her child. I would know it."

"I planned to take an extended vacation out of the country until Kelly was old enough that you would no longer recognize her." He shifted his gaze to Thad. "But this has gone too far now. Put down the gun, Thad."

"I told you already." Thad waved his gun. "I'm the one who will be charged with attempted kidnapping and trying to kill Rachael. I can't survive jail again, and I won't let you turn me in."

"The police are on the way," Rachael warned. "Give up now before murder is added to your crimes."

"No worries." Thad laughed and shoved William hard until his foot landed on the edge of the lake. "I've got it all figured out. The DNA test for Kelly is right on the table in the house. Once the police see William is Kelly's father and find out about his sordid affairs, they'll know he's behind the kidnapping, and when he couldn't get away with it, he dragged you out to the pond and ended both of your lives.

"Now move." He pushed William farther onto the lake.

The sound of cracking ice split the quiet. Rachael glanced at an area of the ice where wind had cleared the snow. A fissure in the ice snaked like a living thing across the clearing.

"Keep moving, William," Thad said.

William peered at Rachael, his face filled with anguish.

"I'm sorry," he said again and took another step.

The cracking sound intensified, and water oozed up through the fracture in the ice.

Rachael's fear skyrocketed.

Thad rested his free hand on his chest and cackled. "Oh, poor me. I came home to check on Gloria. As I drove past, I saw William forcing you out here at gunpoint, I came to see what was going on—and arrived just in time to see the water swallow you both."

SIXTEEN

Jake slammed on his brakes near William's house and opened the storage container in the truck bed. He grabbed a rope and the Mylar thermal blanket he kept for emergencies. He shoved them into his jacket, then hoofed it toward the lake. As he got near, he crept into the woods until he was close enough to see Thad waving his gun. Then his gaze went to Rachael cringing on the lake, water oozing onto the ice a few feet away. She wasn't wearing a jacket, and her arms were wrapped around her middle. William stood closer to shore as if frozen in place.

"Drop your weapon." Skyler's voice suddenly came from behind a tree much closer to Thad.

Surprised, Jake swung his gaze to Skyler, who stood with her gun extended.

Thad spun, his weapon fixed on her. He chambered a round.

Jake aimed his own gun. All officers were taught to put two bullets in the chest of any person threatening life because the chest was a wide target, and the bullets would instantly stop the threat. Jake should have done as he'd been taught, but he didn't want Rachael to live with the trauma of seeing Thad die in front of her.

Jake dropped his finger to the trigger. Pulled. The bullet zipped across the space. Struck Thad's gun hand. His gun fell to the ground, and he cried out.

"It's Jake," he yelled to Skyler so she wouldn't fire on him.

He charged out from cover to tackle Thad as Skyler pounded his way. He took hold of Thad's arms and jerked them behind his back, then slapped on handcuffs. Jake glanced at the bullet wound on Thad's hand and knew he needed to stop the bleeding. But first, Rachael and William needed to be rescued.

Skyler picked up Thad's weapon and shoved it into her jacket pocket.

"Take charge of him," Jake commanded.

Skyler nodded and stood above Thad, her gun trained on him. Her face was still pale, and Jake saw a bit of a tremor in her hands, but she put authority into her tone. "Don't make a move."

Jake heard another crack from the ice rend the air.

"Jake." Panic filled Rachael's voice. "The water is getting higher."

"I know, honey. Hold on. Don't either of you move." He jumped up, pulled the rope from inside his jacket and unfurled it as he ran for the shoreline. He tied a long loop near the end as he locked eyes with William. "Rachael's life depends on you not moving."

William nodded, but Jake had no confidence that if the ice became more unstable, the man wouldn't panic and bolt.

Jake met Rachael's gaze, and his heart constricted at the terror he found there.

"Okay, honey," he said as he tried to battle down his own fear of the water easing up on her feet. "I'm going to throw a rope out to you, and once it reaches you, grab hold of it. Then I'll pull you to safety. Okay?"

"Yes."

He tossed the rope. It went wide and landed too far to the side.

"I'll try again." He pulled it back, and when he felt the cold wetness of the rope, panic threatened to take him down. He tossed the rope again, but the end fell five feet short of reaching Rachael.

He couldn't step any closer to try again, or his weight would instantly break the ice. She'd have to lie down and reach out, which was a dangerous proposition, as any move on her part could split the ice wide open.

Sirens spiraled closer in the background, but this couldn't wait. She could sink before they arrived.

"Okay, honey, I hate to ask this, but I need you to carefully lie down and reach out for the rope." He met her gaze firmly. "Can you do that for me?"

She nodded.

"Don't worry, and stay strong. Once you have the rope, I'll pull you to safety." He spoke confidently, but he wasn't sure if her hands had enough feeling left in them to hold on to the rope.

She slowly lowered herself to the ice. A heartrending crack pierced the air.

She glanced at him, panic fully taking hold in her eyes.

"Reach out, honey!" he shouted. "You can do it."

She raised her arms and clutched the rope. He wanted to jerk her toward him but forced himself to slowly drag her across the snow-covered ice.

"My hands. They're too cold. I can't hold on." She suddenly let go, just as he'd suspected would happen.

"Can you slide your arm though the loop and hoist it over your shoulder?"

She snaked forward on her belly and got the rope over her shoulder.

"Okay, honey, clamp down on your arm, and I'll bring you to safety."

"Hurry, please."

He took the ice-cold rope, pulling it hand over hand until he'd brought her close enough to shore that he could go in after her if needed.

"Okay, William, back away slowly."

He took a few steps. The ice gave way and split.

"Jump, now!" he commanded William, and at the same time Jake leapt ahead for Rachael.

The ice cracked open. His feet sank into chilling water. The shock took his breath, but Rachael was now sinking into the cold grave and his own comfort was unimportant.

He shot forward and swept her up into his arms. She smiled up at him and collapsed like deadweight. Keeping a careful watch on his footing, Jake backed out of the water. He hit solid ground.

Thank you, God, for protecting her. Thank you.

Jake dropped to the snow and settled Rachael on his lap so he could get to his emergency blanket. He wrapped it around them both and struggled to his feet again. They felt like blocks of ice as he moved away from the lake.

"On the ground next to Thad," Jake said to William, who complied without any argument.

Jake reached Skyler and gave her a wry smile. "I wondered if you were ever going to get out of that bathroom."

"Me, too," she said, and he could tell she wasn't too happy about the sickness. He had no idea how she felt about having a baby.

After these last few days, he now knew he'd be overjoyed if he had a wife and a child on the way. He shifted to look at Rachael. She appeared stunned and in shock. He needed to tend to her soon. He jerked his radio from his pocket and ordered the responding officers to come take possession of Thad and William.

"You said you were shot," he reminded her.

"My arm. Just a scratch."

"Is it still bleeding?"

She shook her head. "It's fine."

"Show it to me." Skyler kept her weapon trained on William and Thad as Rachael pushed her arm free of the blanket.

"She's right. The bleeding's stopped," Skyler said. "I'm so sorry I wasn't there for you."

"It's not your fault."

Skyler shook her head. "No one's ever been hurt on my watch."

"Relax, Skyler," Jake said. "You heard Rachael. It's minor." At least he figured if he kept telling himself that, he wouldn't feel the same guilt Skyler was experiencing.

"Exactly," Rachael said, and this time her voice held a bit of enthusiasm.

A trio of officers came barreling through the snow, and they took control of William and Thad.

"Be careful. I've been shot," Thad whined.

"Probably deserved it, then," one of the officers said, and got Thad to his feet. "We've got an EMT outside who'll be glad to put a smiley face bandage on your boo-boo." He jerked him toward the road, and one of the other deputies took William.

Jake marched behind them and peered at Rachael. "How are you doing, honey?"

"Honestly," she said, her voice trembling, "I feel numb."

"That's to be expected. I know you're cold, but is anything else injured besides your arm?"

She shook her head.

By the time they reached the road, the FRS had arrived, and Jake took Rachael straight to the truck, where Darcie stood waiting in the back. He settled Rachael on the long bench and put the blanket over her.

"Get the heat cranked up," Darcie commanded Jake.

He didn't want to step away from Rachael, but he complied, then returned to watch Darcie tend to Rachael.

Darcie studied Rachael's arm. "The bullet just grazed you. Let me grab a bandage and take care of it."

When Darcie got up, Jake moved closer to Rachael. It took everything he was made of not to sweep her into his arms and hold her close, but he didn't know how she would react, as people in shock from such a traumatic incident reacted in different ways. Some wanted comfort and the touch of another human. Some wanted isolation and to be left alone. He had no idea what she wanted or needed, and he would take a moment to figure it out before doing or saying the wrong thing and adding to her trauma.

She didn't respond positively or negatively so he moved even closer. She peered at him as if seeing him but not recognizing him.

He laid his hand on the bench, palm up, an open invitation.

She glanced at it but kept her hands under the blanket.

Okay, then. She didn't want him to comfort her, and he'd respect her wishes, even if he was aching to hold her.

Rachael couldn't really comprehend what had just happened other than that she was alive and her nightmare had ended. Thanks to Jake and Detective Hunter, who'd asked Rachael to call her Skyler. Two heroes risking their own lives to save hers.

"I recommend a trip to the ER to have this checked

out." Darcie knelt at Rachael's feet and finished wrapping the bandage around her arm.

"Later." Rachael fixed her gaze on Jake, who was talking with a PPB detective just outside the door.

"Have you told him how you feel?" Darcie asked.

Rachael whipped her head around to stare at Darcie.

"Don't look so surprised." Darcie chuckled. "You may not think we can see what's going on between you two, but the whole team can see it."

"I…"

"Yeah," Darcie said. "You're not sure of what you're feeling. I get that. Happened to me with Noah, too. And right now you've got the added shock of what just transpired, and you must have a ton of emotions flooding through your body."

"Exactly," Rachael replied, though honestly, at the moment, other than gratitude to Skyler and Jake, she felt empty inside.

Why the emptiness, she had no idea. Maybe it was because the danger had passed and a Christmas wreath hanging from a wall hook reminded her that she had another holiday alone to look forward to. Many evenings alone in her future, too.

She sighed, but then firmed her shoulders.

She'd been alone on Christmas Eve before. Had been alone every night in the last few years, when she hadn't been babysitting. And she would continue to be alone until she figured out what she wanted her future to hold.

Jake pulled his truck up to the emergency room entrance. He didn't know how he was going to handle another silent drive with Rachael, but he suspected she'd be no more eager to talk now than when he'd brought her in. She'd refused to ride in an ambulance, so Jake had offered to drive her to the ER, assuming they could talk on the way. But she'd curled up in the corner of the truck and stared out the window. He'd asked if she wanted to talk about the incident.

She shook her head and said, "Will someone be giving Pam and Kelly a ride home today?"

"Brady's taking care of it."

"Good," she'd said, and had returned to staring out the window.

Darcie had told him Rachael wasn't experiencing a clinical case of shock. Otherwise he would have been concerned that that was the reason she'd retreated. Or maybe he wanted it to be the reason, as it hurt to think she just didn't want to talk to him.

Jake shifted into Park and climbed out as the hospital doors slid open, and a young man wheeled Rachael out. She stepped from the chair before Jake could get around the truck. He opened the door, and she gave him a tight smile of thanks. They drove in complete silence, but at least this time Rachael wasn't slumped next to the door.

At her house, he walked her up the sidewalk and waited while she unlocked the door. "Would you like me to come in and help clean up the mess from our forensics staff?"

She shook her head. "All I want to do is make a cup of tea and then get a good night's sleep for once."

She was shutting him out. Totally and completely. The ache in his chest felt like the moment the bullets had slammed into his vest. "You'll call me if you need anything?"

She nodded and stepped inside. "Thank you, Jake, for everything you've done for me. And especially what you've done for Pam and Kelly. We are all in your debt."

"You're welcome. I…" His voice trailed off. He didn't

want to let her go, but he knew he had to respect her desire for privacy. "Sleep well, honey."

He turned and walked away, leaving his heart at the door with her.

EPILOGUE

Three days had passed since Rachael had seen Jake, and it was now Christmas Eve. Snow fell heavily outside, blanketing the world in a new beginning. Restless, Rachael prowled her house to relieve her nervousness. She'd invited Pam and Kelly to spend the night with her, but Pam had contacted her parents, and it turned out they wanted to see her but were hurt that she'd shut them out of her life.

She'd since then reconciled with them, and they were spending the holidays together. Of course, her father hadn't had a thing to do with trying to kidnap the baby, but had lied about being home because he was meeting with his lawyer to figure out a way to get visitation rights with Kelly. Now that the family had reunited with Pam, they had no need to pursue those plans. What a blessing their reunion was. It made Rachael smile even now, when she couldn't relax. She was just so unsettled and craved company.

Gloria wasn't available either as she'd gone to stay with her parents, where she'd have their support in getting her recent drinking problem under control. She vowed to return and take over CAR to make sure it survived the scandal, and Rachael looked forward to working with her friend again. Both William and Thad had been charged with various counts of kidnapping and attempted murder and were in jail awaiting trial.

It seemed like things had been settled for most everyone except her. Maybe that was the reason for her unease tonight. She felt driven to do something, but she didn't know what. She had to find a way to keep busy.

The center. There were still things she could do to prepare for her visit from the licensing rep on New Year's Eve day. Yes, that was it. Cleaning would keep her busy.

She grabbed her jacket and stepped out the door. Still uneasy after her life had so recently been threatened, she took a quick look around.

"Relax," she whispered, and changed her focus to the positive. She forced herself to keep remembering that though she'd lost her family, she was still alive, and God had plans for her.

She stepped through the snow, which made the outdoors a winter wonderland. Her thoughts traveled to the firehouse, and she knew how perfect it would look tonight with the fresh snow and Skyler's lights twinkling off the glistening whiteness.

She'd tried not to think of Jake the past few days and wonder what he was doing for the holiday, but her mind kept going to him. She assumed the entire team was gathered together in the family room with stockings filled, the fireplace lit and colored lights glowing on the big tree. The room would be overflowing with laughter and love. Maybe Skyler had even told everyone she was pregnant, and they were celebrating with her and Logan.

Tears came to Rachael's eyes, and she swiped them away to concentrate on driving. She wasn't about to blind herself and run off snow-covered roads to be stranded in a ditch on Christmas Eve. If she did, she'd have to take people away from their loved ones to help her out, and she would hate to do that.

She crept along slowly and turned into the center parking lot, a perfect blanket of white when it should have been covered with little footsteps coming and going for the day.

She sighed and got out. The outside light shone on the shrubs in their white coverings, painting a lovely picture and cheering her up a bit. She slipped inside. In her office, she plugged in a miniature Christmas tree that her staff had given her last year and hoped her attitude would improve.

Instead, the tiny twinkling lights simply reminded her that her staff and the center families were all likely gathered with their own families. The thought made her feel so alone.

She dropped onto her chair and glanced around. She'd once thought of the center as her sanctuary. A place to recover from her loss. But tonight? Her commitment to the center families hadn't changed, but at the end of the day, the children went home with their parents, leaving her behind.

Jake's face the night of the fund-raiser came to mind. She'd told him to let the past go. To live life again. She hadn't taken her own advice, the very reason she sat here by herself, unhappy and brooding. She was so tired of living this way. She'd nearly come to the end of her life at Gloria's house, and now it was clear that she had reached the end of what she could do for herself.

She dropped to her knees, folded her hands and rested

her head on them, her thoughts on how something had to give so she could move on.

"Father," she said. "I want to change. Please…please help me."

Rachael's car sat in the center parking lot, and Jake's heart soared. He'd first stopped at her house, but when he didn't find her at home, he'd hoped she'd be here. He didn't have an idea of what he would say to her, but just like he needed to breathe, he had to talk to her.

He hadn't seen her in three days, and he could focus on nothing else. Not even work. He finally admitted to himself that he needed her in his life. What that meant, he wasn't sure, but he wanted to start by inviting her to spend Christmas Eve with the team.

On the keypad, he punched the security code she'd previously given him, and the lock gave a satisfying click. Inside, he paused to take off his jacket and heard Rachael's voice drifting out of her office.

Did she have company? If so, he wouldn't intrude.

He peeked around the corner to discover she wasn't talking to someone; she was praying. She asked for help to let go of her guilt over the loss of her husband and child.

Jake's heart creased with her pain. He'd given his guilt to God, and for the past few days he'd actually stopped worrying about life. He knew he would still struggle at times, but he was thrilled she was trying to do the same thing. It was time for both of them to stop investing their entire lives in other people, and have lives of their own, too.

He waited until she finished her prayer, then said, "Knock, knock."

He startled her, and she jumped.

"Sorry to scare you." He dropped down next to her and took her hands. "I've missed you."

"Me, too." She looked away shyly.

He gently turned her face to look at him. "I love you, Rachael."

She gaped at him.

"I think we can let go of our pasts and make a wonderful life together," he rushed on before she shut him down. "What do you think?"

"I think…" she said and fell silent for a moment. "I love you, too. So much." She freed her hand and gently touched his cheek, sending waves of emotions flooding through him.

"I was a fool for letting guilt over losing my family ruin my life." He paused and took her hands again. "I'm convinced God brought you into my life to help me let it go."

"Ditto for me."

His heart soared. "If we take things one day at a time and don't worry about anything beyond that, we'll be fine."

Jake got up and drew her to her feet. He settled his arms around her back.

She stood on tiptoe and wrapped her arms around his neck. She met his gaze, and the love he'd never thought he'd see in a woman's eyes shone up at him. He didn't hesitate, but lowered his head and settled his lips on hers. Heat traveled through his body, and he knew deep in his heart that he'd never be cold again.

* * *

"Wait, what?" Rachael asked as Jake pulled his truck to the curb. "You said a surprise, and I thought you meant at the firehouse."

"You assumed that, and I wasn't about to correct you so it could be more of a surprise." He grinned at her. "You'll want to zip up your coat and put your gloves on."

"We're going outside?"

He nodded.

"This is *so* not fair," she said, but she was loving every minute of the lighthearted feel between them.

After they'd kissed—oh, that enchanting, wonderful kiss—he'd grabbed her coat, hurried her into it and then rushed her into his truck. To go to the firehouse, he'd said, but now he'd pulled over on a side street about a mile away.

He jumped out, then came to open her door. "Are you ready for your surprise?"

She eagerly nodded, but butterflies filled her stomach. He took her hand and helped her down from the truck. He kept a tight hold and walked her to the corner. The powdery snow swooshed over her feet and glistened in the reflection of colored lights on trees and homes in the area, adding to the stillness and the feeling of mystery he'd created.

They reached the corner, and he turned her to face him. "Close your eyes, and your surprise will be in front of you before you know it."

She clamped her eyes closed, and he took her hands to lead her around the corner.

He soon came to a stop. "Okay, you can open your eyes."

She slowly lifted her lids, and delight captured her

when she spotted a horse-drawn carriage parked at the curb. A large chestnut horse pawed his hoofs in the snow as a driver sat behind him on a bright red sleigh with holly painted on the sides. It was decorated with fresh pine boughs and sparkling lights.

"When you first saw the firehouse, you said the place would be perfect if you could arrive in a sleigh. I wanted the night to be perfect for you, so…" He gestured at the sleigh.

She stared up at him in wonder. "You remembered."

"I remember everything about you." He moved close and trailed his finger down her face. "And that's why I couldn't stay away."

Staring up at him, she got lost in his eyes and didn't want the moment ever to end.

The driver cleared his throat.

Jake glanced at him. "Oh, right. Sorry, Stan." He turned back to Rachael. "Stan and I go way back, and I finally talked him into coming out tonight, but he does have a family to get back to, so…" Jake bowed and held out his arm. "Your carriage awaits, my lady."

She was smiling so wide she thought her face might crack, but she couldn't stop as Jake helped her into the sleigh. He settled next to her, not a hairbreadth between them, and covered their legs with a fuzzy blanket.

As the sleigh jolted ahead, the scent of pine and horse and Jake's soap mixed into a memory she would never forget. She laid her head on his shoulder, and they rode to the firehouse in silence, the only sounds her beating heart, the clip-clop of hooves and the swish of snow over the runners.

When they turned the corner to the firehouse, she sat forward. The driveway and yard were pristine and white. The lights twinkled and glistened on the snow as she'd imagined, but she'd never expected to see the entire FRS team and their families standing outside and waving at them.

She didn't think after seeing the sleigh that her heart could be any fuller, but now it overflowed with joy and love and gratitude, everything a Christmas season could bring.

Stan stopped the sleigh, and Jake helped her down, then introduced people she hadn't met before. Krista's grandfather, Otto, was first, his chubby red cheeks glowing with health and vitality.

"Ach, it's good to see someone smiling so much," he said and gave her a quick hug. "It does an old man's heart good to see such joy."

Next Archer stepped forward to introduce his fiancée, Emily, who in turn introduced her aunt Birdie, a woman whose outlandish attire made her look like a throwback to the sixties.

"Nice to meet you," Birdie said and settled an arm around Emily's shoulder.

"Why are we standing out here in the cold when there's cocoa and cider waiting for us inside?" Darcie asked and started shooing them all inside.

When they stepped in, Woof barked and jumped between everyone's legs, trying to figure out what all the excitement was about.

Darcie stopped near the kitchen island covered with mugs, empty trays and serving dishes. "Grab a drink, we'll make our annual toast, then have dinner."

"We gather around the tree, and Jake says a few words," Skyler whispered to Rachael as she tugged her to a stop and faced her. "But this year I plan to upstage him. Seems like he won't notice, though. He only has eyes for you, and I can see the feeling is mutual."

Rachael nodded.

"I hope there aren't any bad feelings between us. I know I was hard on you—"

"I've forgotten all about it," Rachael interrupted. "I want you to do the same. I let guilt ruin several years of my life, so promise me you won't do the same thing."

"Okay, good. Yes, you've got my word."

Rachael gave Skyler a hug, and she seemed surprised and discomfited by it.

"Skyler's not much of a hugger," Jake said, offering Rachael a steaming cup of hot cocoa with mini marshmallows melting on top. "C'mon. The others are already at the tree."

He took her free hand, and they joined the group. Rachael spotted the kindly Otto talking with Pilar, their eyes alight with interest in each other. Rachael didn't say anything to Jake, but she couldn't wait to see what developed between the pair.

"Thank you all for coming tonight," Jake said.

"Like we had a choice," Cash grumbled good-naturedly, and Krista rolled her eyes.

"Pipe down, dude," Brady warned. "The longer we talk, the longer it is before we can eat Darcie's Christmas Eve feast."

Archer lifted a brow. "You guys are giving Rachael a bad impression."

"Trust me," Darcie said. "After spending a few days here, she already knows what a bunch of clowns you guys are."

The team members laughed good-naturedly, and Rachael joined in, already feeling like part of the family.

"Before Jake has his say…" Skyler took Logan's hand, then led him to the front of the group. "We have an announcement to make."

Logan wrapped his arm around his wife, his face beaming with happiness.

She peered up at him. "I'm pregnant, and our child is due in early summer."

The room erupted in clapping and shouts of congratulations. When they quieted down, Jake said, "Congratulations, but this is old news to me."

"You knew and didn't tell us?" Morgan cried out.

"Yes, how could you?" Emily said.

His fellow teammates descended on him, chastising him for not telling them, either.

Jake escaped their clutches and little Isabel broke away from Pilar to approach him, a frown on her face.

"Can we please eat so we can open presents?" she asked, her eyes hopeful.

"Absolutely, little one." Jake ruffled her hair and turned to the group. "Isabel wants to eat, so we are adjourned."

More chaos filled the space as everyone moved toward the dining room. Rachael enjoyed the laughter, the conversations. It was all perfection that, if not for God's grace, she would be missing out on right now.

Jake turned to her and circled his arms around her. "Are you sure you want to become a part of this crazy ready-made family?"

She smiled up at him, making sure every ounce of love she felt for him was in her gaze. "It's perfect. Everything is perfect. Especially my Christmas gift."

"You mean the sleigh ride? That's not your gift. I got you something else."

She raised her hands around his neck and drew his head closer.

"Turns out," she whispered for his ears only, "you're the only gift I wanted all along."

* * * * *

Don't miss these other FIRST RESPONDERS *stories from Susan Sleeman:*

SILENT NIGHT STANDOFF
EXPLOSIVE ALLIANCE
HIGH-CALIBER HOLIDAY
EMERGENCY RESPONSE
SILENT SABOTAGE

Find more great reads at www.LoveInspired.com.

Dear Reader,

All good things come to an end, they say, and I hope that you have found the First Responders series a good thing. The series certainly has been a good thing in my life. I loved getting to know each of these characters and sharing their struggles with you as they searched for love in their lives, and I am sad to see the series end.

I am contented that all these special characters have found people to share their lives with, and that they've also found peace in their lives. If you've ever struggled for peace, I hope these stories have helped you see that God's peace is right there waiting for you, and you just have to reach out and grab it.

If you'd like to learn more about my other books, please stop by my website at www.susansleeman.com. I also love hearing from readers, so please contact me via email, susan@susansleeman.com, or on my Facebook page, www.Facebook.com/SusanSleemanBooks, or write to me c/o Love Inspired, HarperCollins, 24th floor, 195 Broadway, New York, NY 10007.

Blessings,
Susan Sleeman

Zane Scofield stared through his high-powered binoculars, scanning the hills and mountains all around him. For the last day or so, he'd had the strange sense that they were being watched. Who had been stalking them and why?

He saw movement through his binoculars and focused in. Several ATVs were headed down the mountain toward the campsite where he'd left Heather alone. He zeroed in and saw the handmade flag. He knew that flag. His mind was sucked back in time seven years ago to when he had lived in these mountains as a scared seventeen-year-old. If this was who he thought it was, Heather was in danger.

He could hear the ATVs drawing closer, but not coming directly into the camp. They were headed a little deeper into the forest. He ran toward the mechanical sound, pushing past the rising fear.

He called for Heather only once. He stopped to listen.

He heard her call back—faint and far away, repeating his name. He ran in the direction of the sound with his rifle still slung over his shoulder. When he came to the clearing, he saw a boy not yet in his teens throwing rocks into a hole and screaming, "Shut up. Be quiet."

Zane held his rifle up toward the boy. He could never shoot a child, but maybe the threat would be enough.

The kid grew wide-eyed and snarled at him. "More men are coming. So there." Then the boy darted into the forest, yelling behind him, "You won't get away."

Zane ran over to the hole. Heather gazed up at him, relief spreading across her face.

Voices now drifted through the trees, men on foot headed this way.

Zane grabbed an evergreen bough and stuck it in the hole for Heather to grip. She climbed agilely and quickly. He grabbed her hand and pulled her the rest of the way out. "We have to get out of here."

There was no time to explain the full situation to her. His worst nightmare coming true, his past reaching out to pull him into a deep dark hole. The past he thought he'd escaped.

If Willis was back in the high country, he needed to get Heather to safety and fast. He knew what Willis was capable of. Their lives depended on getting out of the high country.

Don't miss
BIG SKY SHOWDOWN
by Sharon Dunn, available wherever
Love Inspired® Suspense books and ebooks are sold.

www.LoveInspired.com

LISEXP1216

Turn your love of reading into rewards you'll love with
Harlequin My Rewards